LAIR

LAIR
1

D.V. SULLIVAN

TRANSMARINIA PRESS

ISBN for ebook: 979-8-9866781-1-5
ISBN for paperback: 979-8-9866781-0-8
LCCN: 2023900440
First Published 2023, 2nd Edition 2024

For readers 18+. Contains brief descriptions of domestic violence.

Cover design by Trif Book Design.

Transmarinia Press
2709 N Hayden Island Dr
STE 330550
Portland, OR 97217

*If you were ever made to feel
you weren't enough,
this is for you*

ONE

It was 2:59 a.m. and I laid rigid in bed, listening to Josh breathe. Waiting.

The next part was the hardest: to actually start. To make the decision to leave Josh and set aside our old life together, packed away like so much treasure, and confront the reality of a future that would not contain him. Not include Josh.

The digital numbers on my clock changed: 3:00. Time to go.

And still I laid there, trembling. How could I go on? How could I do this?

Then I thought of the reddish-black bruises on my cheek, and my jaw ached as it clenched.

3:01.

I pulled the covers away, and there was his meaty arm draped over me. I gingerly lifted it, not daring to breathe, and set it aside. Then the horrifying moment of scooching out, my weight depressing the bed.

He snorted in his sleep, and I froze. But he only turned away and heaved a sigh.

Jesus.

My one bag was already packed and waiting for me under the bed, and I knew Cailee would be waiting for me. So that was all taken care of.

Next, tiptoeing over the broken glass and dirty laundry on the floor, careful to not look at the fist-sized hole in the wall. The terror pouring out of me in rivulets of sweat. A squeak of the floor as I dipped to grab my coat and shoes.

My hand was shaking when I laid it on the doorknob. My breath held as I waited to hear if he stirred, never daring to look back.

Then I slipped out, like a grave robber, into the night.

The farmyard was lush and green in the Oregon darkness. A light rain pattered down, and the sweet smell of the stables stung my nostrils. I had begun to shake by that point; I was in a bad way. But I didn't have time for that. I was not yet in the clear. I had crushed sleeping pills into Bowser's food earlier that evening, and he was still in his doghouse by the door, snout on paws, chain coiled before him. But I didn't trust him sleeping for long. Not only was that black rottweiler big as hell, he was also blindly loyal to Josh and hated me with an evil will.

I swallowed and snuck past. Ahead, gleaming in the rain at the end of the drive with its headlights off, Cailee's crappy pickup waited in a cloud of exhaust. So close.

My insides turned. Maybe this would actually happen.

The low growl behind me shattered that hope.

I turned to see Bowser standing with heavy muscles corded under his sleek black coat, slobber dripping from his snarled lips. His pinprick eyes blazed death.

Cailee stuck her head out the driver side window. "Run, Arie! Run!"

I bolted. There was a heart-stopping unsnaking of chain, and then an angry clink as Bowser was jerked short, teeth snapping shut inches behind me.

His ferocious barking brought the lights of the farmhouse on, and my knees threatened to give out.

"Hurry! Hurry!" Cailee shrieked.

I couldn't help it: I looked back. And there was that familiar shape, a dark shadow that stomped out into the yard, hands balled into fists. "Get back here, you bitch!"

Sobbing as I scrambled into the truck and slammed the door shut behind me. As the truck peeled out in rooster tails of gravel, the figure pounding on my window, making me shriek. My hands to my ears, but the voice getting through all the same. "You'll never do better than me! You hear me? You don't deserve it. You're mine!*"*

And he was right. That was the terrible thing. This was all for me to make a life for myself, to reclaim an existence where what I ate, what I said, what I thought was not controlled by someone else.

But what was I to care about now? How would I know I was alive?

His lasting gift to me. The knowledge that I could run all I want, but how would I ever replace him? Who else could ever pose so vibrant a challenge?

And the truck barreled on through the wet night, the shadow of my old life falling impossibly behind, and Cailee rubbed my back and made soothing noises as the rain pounded and the darkness flew up to swallow me and—

I tip up my face and drink in the sun's warmth, memories leaching away. Even after two weeks in the shimmering tropicality of Florida, I haven't gotten used to it. The perpetual rain of Oregon has turned me into a sunshine addict.

A cool shadow crosses my face and I open my eyes—Cailee stands above me, hands on hips, her perfect brow wrinkled in annoyance. "You haven't heard a word I've said, have you?"

"Sorry," I mumble, dipping my scrub brush into the sudsy water bucket. "What were you saying?"

It's June. We're in the Port of Miami, on a little wooden cruiser that's all gleaming mahogany and pinstriped topsides. There are rows of these classic-looking, Venetian-style boats bobbing at the docks, and we have to clean all of them today. Daywork, they call it. What we aspiring yachties do for income while we hope to get a position aboard a boat.

"I *said*," Cailee intones, "what do you think about Greg?"

I glance over at Greg on the next boat over, one of the many bland-looking hotties who's in the crew house with us in Fort Lauderdale. He catches my eye and grins, and I look away.

"Mm-mm," I grunt noncommittally.

Cailee pinches off the hose she's using to wash down the deck. "Aurora Strand. I helped you escape your abusive ex by bringing you with me into the glamorous world of yachting. The least you can do is help me get laid."

I sigh and give her a look. Point taken.

"Okay. How about Jordan?"

To my surprise, Cailee blushes. "Well . . ."

I gape. "Cailee. Don't tell me you already . . ."

Cailee shrugs, one of those helpless little gestures she's perfected.

"Oh my God," I laugh. "Was it . . . back at the crew house?"

The crew house. Basically an off-the-grid condo for yachties. And I do mean off-the-grid. The owner blacked out the windows and demands we enter from the back so we don't draw the attention of the hotel chains, who hate crew houses for avoiding hotel tax laws.

Also, they're a notorious place for hookups.

"No," Cailee blushes again. "We kinda . . ." And she points through the window of the wheelhouse to the hidden interior of the boat.

My jaw drops. "Cailee Summers, you little slut. You did it while you were *dayworking?*"

Another helpless shrug. *You know you still love me . . .*

"But . . ." I splutter. "How . . .?"

Cailee gets a mischievous little grin on her face and plants one foot on the foredeck of the neighboring boat a few feet over, so she's straddling both. "I tried this little move . . ." And she bends forward as if to hose down the boat's hull, showing off perfectly toned legs and ass cheeks poking out of tiny cut-off shorts. A blinking advertisement that screams "FUCK THIS."

Greg freezes, mop poised and eyes huge.

Cailee flips her wavy blonde hair and looks over her shoulder at me, brow arched.

We both burst out laughing. It feels good. Needed. Because for a second there I was beginning to think about my ex again.

This is why I love Cailee: She's impervious. Her trust—in flings, in romance—is total. She pursues a guy wholeheartedly, miseries be damned, and always survives without a scratch. In the throes of it she's unabashed, full of cringing mushiness, of almost willful destruction, appalling to watch. But when it is clear it's not working—the door shuts. No wavering for her, no drawn-out, humiliating uncertainties. She is brisk and uproarious, pragmatic and breathlessly objective about it all, unapologetic about the spectacle she's made of herself.

In other words, she couldn't be more different from myself.

Me, who stuck with the same guy since I was sixteen. Who had thought this farmer's son with the stocky frame and sensitive reddish skin was my soulmate. I had thought, in the beginning, that he was perfect. I had never felt so seen, so cared for. I put him on a pedestal. Yes, I quickly saw—even if he did not—that he was a delicate man, and considered it part of my duty as his partner to accommodate that insecurity. Little did I know how slippery a slope that would prove to be. Why not put off going to college in the city for a few years to support his dream of running a farm? Why not put up with his touchiness about being contradicted, his tendency to shift blame onto me if his flaws were exposed, if his ego happened to be as sensitive as his skin? Why burden him with my thoughts and feelings if he was so busy? Why not hide from my friends how I felt like a hostage at the farmhouse when he was drunk, and what he'd sometimes do to me? No one wanted to hear about that.

It was the price of loving him, I told myself. This was how he needed to be loved.

Cailee disagreed.

And so, after spending a year wearing me down and planning our escape, she had dragged me here. To the Sunshine State.

Free at last, at the suddenly ancient-sounding age of twenty-four, and feeling like I don't know the first thing about myself.

Sensing my thoughts, Cailee pulls out her phone and hunkers down beside me. "Guess who has a million followers now?"

I sigh and look at the Instagram feed: Emmie Gallagher. A blonde-haired beauty in a bikini with puffy lips and those pushed-out come-on-me tits that just beg for male attention. Of course, she's hanging on some businessman's arm on a yacht, and a twinge of jealousy pinches my heart. It's hard not to compare myself to her. I'm brunette, short, compact, un-plumped—hardly supermodel material.

I shake my head. "Can you believe she graduated high school with us?"

"A bona fide Influencer. Only took her a couple of months. You think she's banging that guy?"

"Definitely." I pause. "But still. It'd be nice to enjoy the good life."

Cailee turns thoughtful. "Yeah . . ." For a moment she scrolls through endless photos of Emmie frolicking in exotic locales, then shoves her phone back in her shorts. "We'll get there. We're both getting staffed on superyachts and seeing the world. Right?" She holds out her pinky, and I laugh and crook mine around it.

"Right."

"And then we'll seduce the billionaire owners and retire at twenty-five."

I snort and push her. "That's what *you'll* be doing."

Cailee smirks and stands, grabbing the hose. "Suit yourself, Goody Two-Shoes."

Smiling, I look around. Boats bob, gulls cry, fresh-faced dockwalkers pad down the floating links of docks, hoping to score a gig to the Med. Behind us, hot-pink Art Deco buildings and glass-plated skyscrapers shimmer in the heat, the flamboyant architectural magic of Miami. Sometimes I don't know how I got here, or into what world I've strayed. I could be content here. This could be enough.

I shut my eyes—

RRR. RRR. RRR. I jerk and pull out my phone, check the incoming call: *Unknown.* My heart sinks. The blood thumps in my wrists. How did he find me? How did Josh—

But Cailee knows exactly what I'm thinking.

"It can't be him," she mollifies. "You got a new number, remember?" I look up into her eyes, and find enough strength there to nod and take the call.

"Hello?"

A cool, clipped voice drifts into my ear. "Miss Strand?"

I feel the hairs on the back of my neck prick and glance over at Cailee. "Yes?"

"This is Renata Sproule with Lair Yachting Incorporated. I have a captain who'd like to speak with you."

I put a hand to my brow. "I'm sorry. Who is this?"

"Lair Yachting Incorporated. I have a captain who'd like to speak with you in person."

"In person." I lift my brows. Both Cailee and Greg are watching me now, hose and mop gripped tight.

"Can you be here in two hours?"

"I, uh . . ." I look over at Cailee, and she frantically motions at me: *Yes! Yes! Do it!*

"Yeah, sure. No problem."

"Perfect. See you soon, Miss Strand."

Click.

I stare at my phone like an idiot. What just happened?

"Well?" Cailee's patience lasts all of three seconds. "Did you get an interview?"

A little bubble of happiness is expanding inside me. My voice comes out hollow and stunned. "Yeah. With Lair Yachting Incorporated."

Cailee and Greg look at each other, and I feel my stomach twist.

"What?"

A big breath, and Cailee says, "Did you know anything about Lair Yachting when you sent them your résumé?"

I shake my head.

"They're, like . . ." Another glance, and Greg takes over.

"They're a crew agency who work exclusively for the biggest names in the yachting industry. Like, the *mega-rich*. It's, I don't know, a mysterious club or something."

"Arie." Cailee fixes me with her gaze. "You just won the yachting lottery." And a huge, dazzling smile spreads across her face. "So go nail this interview already."

Excitement buzzes in my chest like bees. I jump up and down, hands fluttering. "Oh my God, oh my God!"

Cailee laughs and points. "Go! *Go!*"

I hop onto the dock. "What do I do? What do I wear?"

Cailee talks me down like a paramedic. "Go back to the crew house. Get a fresh polo and your navy skirt—"

"What about the daywork here? I haven't—"

"Are you *kidding* me?" Cailee snorts. "This is a once-in-a-lifetime opportunity, and you want to throw it away for some fucking *daywork*?" She makes a shooing motion. "*Go.*"

Melting with gratitude, I whirl about . . . and bump right into a soft wall of flesh: Randy, our boss for the day, a garden-variety rich redneck Floridouche who lives alone in an empty Italianate marble mansion, eats fast food every day and wears shorts and a baseball cap. His eyes bug in his tanned oil rigger's face. "Where do you think *you're* goin'? These boats look done to you?"

I quail. "I—I'm sorry. I have an interview. I can't pass it up—"

Randy turns puce. "You know you won't get a red fucking dime if you leave now. You seriously walking out on me?"

I glance over my shoulder: Cailee and Greg shake their heads. *Don't you dare wuss out.*

I turn back, my jaw hardening. "Yeah," I say, trembling, and force my voice steady. "Yeah, I guess I am." And pulling the spare rags out of my shorts pockets, I throw them down on the dock and brush past a shellshocked Randy.

I can't help but grin as Cailee and Greg's cheers echo in my ears.

Greg lets me borrow his Jeep for my drive back to Fort Lauderdale. More like my flight. The Jeep roars down the winding, elevated highways at a frenzied pace, and even so I'm barely within the two hours when I get there. I sit in the Jeep staring at the building for a long moment. It's not like the other boxy, glossy-looking crew agencies lining Southeast 17th Street. This one seems old. Tucked away between other modern-looking storefronts, it reminds me of a toadstool shrinking from the heat, its modest terra cotta and stucco façade hailing from the days of Spanish colonialism. Above the door the words in Gothic typeface: LAIR YACHTING, INC.

How strange.

I inspect myself in the Jeep's rearview mirror. My coal-black hair is pulled back into a tight ponytail, my green-flecked hazel eyes only somewhat baggy from fatigue. I haven't sweated through my crisp white polo, so that's something. Hopping out, I smooth down the navy skirt I've hastily changed into. At least I look the part.

Let's do this.

A bell tinkles as I slip through the door, and a stale dimness greets me. For a moment I stand there, eyes straining at the sharp contrast from the blazing sun outside. No lights are on in here, and the blinds of the large window fronting the street are fully drawn, casting the agency in a deep gloom. Have they moved? Are they even open? I squint to make out a waiting room with vintage posters of far-flung destinations on the walls. VISIT MOROCCO! VISIT ROMANIA! SEE THE CAVES OF SARDINIA! The last features an illustration of bats fluttering out into an evening sky.

I think, *I have made a mistake here.*

"Hello?" I hazard into the dark, forearms prickling. "Miss Strand?"

I leap into the air, letting out a little shriek as I press a hand to the middle of my chest.

There's a woman. A woman behind a receptionist's desk, just sitting there in the dark. I let a gush of air out of my lungs. "I'm sorry, I didn't see you there—"

But heels are clicking toward me, and before I can gather myself Renata Sproule is smiling down at me, her platinum A-line bob gleaming like a helmet in the gloom. Her teeth and black skirt are flawless. It's only the mole riding on one cheekbone and the shocking paleness of her skin which somehow communicate to me an air of immoral dealings, sinister intent.

"Yes," she says, in a vague accent that hints at European origins. "We like to keep it dim in here. The heat. It's ghastly, isn't it?"

Ghastly.

What an odd word. An old word.

But her antiquated formality extends further. She bows slightly, holding out one hand in a queer gesture of hospice. There's an office back there.

"Please," Renata Sproule says in that indefinable accent. "The captain will be with you shortly."

TWO

I sit in a hard mahogany chair in the dim office and wait as the captain studies my résumé. He's wearing a white epaulette shirt that shows he's still powerfully built for a man in his fifties, his silver hair swept back from the broad, glowering forehead of a man who has seen everything, and found it lacking. Including my résumé.

I'm not good at waiting.

Sure, I fit the image of a yachtie to a T. But after hearing of Lair Yachting, Inc. (and that shadowy run-in with the receptionist), my throat has gone dry.

Perhaps the captain knows this yachting thing isn't just an adventure for me—it's a crisis. How many girls has he seen running from broken homes or broken men, hoping to reinvent themselves on the high seas? Too many, it would seem. His eyes glide over me with practiced precision, lingering on the fading bruise on my cheek I was not wholly successful in hiding with concealer. I lift my chin and force myself to meet his eyes.

Captain Redfearn opens his mouth and speaks. "You have freckles."

I blink, feeling my ears grow hot. "Uh, yeah," I stammer. "I do."

The captain frowns. "He doesn't like freckles," he mutters, and as my thoughts spiral at that he adds, eyeing my hair, "Would you mind changing your appearance? If requested?"

I feel a coldness seep into me. "Uh, sure. I mean, no. I wouldn't mind."

The captain absently nods and glances back down at my résumé. I don't know what for. There's nothing there but a few basic training courses I crammed into the last couple of weeks: the STCW, a smattering of classes on stewardess competency, and an ENG1 or seafarer medical certificate. A glorified crash course on maritime survival and how to be a slave to the fabulously wealthy.

"Bartending experience is good," Captain Redfearn ventures. "How many years as a manager?"

"Three."

A nod. That's a win. "And is that the sum total of your service experience?"

My ears grow hot again. I consider mentioning teaching a children's yoga class at the local Y back in Oregon and decide against it. "There . . . weren't exactly a lot of options where I lived. I was basically out in cow country."

This, I immediately know, is a mistake. Captain Redfearn's eyes flick at me over the top of the paper. "You do know that in this industry, the expectation is for the best service in the world, right? Forget your quotidian

CEOs, forget royalty. Yachting is for people who shit in gold toilets and have never seen a cow in their life, and they always—*always*—expect perfection. Can you give them that?"

My throat has suddenly contracted. "Yes," I squeak.

The captain leans back in his chair and examines me with hard gray eyes. "If a guest got a bloodstain on their twenty thousand-dollar silk blouse, how would you get it out?"

"Um . . ."

"Who do you serve first, a guest or his wife?"

I bite my lip.

The captain sighs, a huff of cool disappointment. "Mr. Voper does not care for unsophisticated country girls."

The old-world name sends a shiver down my spine. "Look, I'm a fast learner—"

But the captain is standing. "You're not what we're looking for—"

"Please!" He freezes, and we both stare at my hand that's flown on top of his. I remove it. "Please," I say again, more quietly. "I can't—go back. To where I came from." My voice begins to quiver as I get a flash of a familiar, sneering face—*You think you're better than me?*—and I fight it, continuing in steely composure, "I have nothing. I spent everything I had to get here. If I don't get this, I don't know what I'll do."

Perhaps it's the raw urgency in my voice, or simply the blatant desperation—but he settles back in his seat, cocks his head and folds his hands. "All right, then," he says. "Stand up. Let's get a look at you."

I feel my stomach bottom out. "What?"

The corner of his mouth curls in a faint smirk. "Mr. Voper is very . . . *particular* . . . about the type of girl who works on his boat." He gestures to the middle of the room. "Please."

Heat sweeps up my chest, my neck, into my face. My hands, I find, are shaking as I stand and smooth my skirt. Is this legal? This can't be legal. My head is a buzzing cloud of confusion as I tuck a flyaway hair behind my ear and turn to face him, feeling like a child.

He has his phone out and is pointing it at me. *Click.*

He's taken a picture.

What the . . . ?

Before I can say a word, the phone's vanished. He stands, résumé in hand. "I'll pass these on to Mr. Voper," he says curtly, and extends a meaty hand. "Thank you for coming in."

The dismissal rings in the air. I shake the hand in a daze, murmur some thank you and grope out, right past Renata Sproule sitting with unnerving content in the dark behind her receptionist's desk. "Mind the heat," she trills as the bell tinkles behind me, and then I'm squinting in the glare outside as my mind processes with awful clarity: *What the fuck was that?* What am I to do now? Will I run out of money before I find a job? I reach out to steady myself on Greg's Jeep as the final, crushing thought comes: Will I get weak enough and go back to—

"Miss Strand."

I whirl—it is, impossibly, the captain standing in front of me, phone in hand as if just hanging up from a call. With no change in expression whatsoever he stares at me and says, "Congratulations. You'll be on the first flight to Monaco tomorrow."

"I hate you," Cailee whines as she punches my shoulder with a beer, and I salute her with my own. "Love you too, babe."

Greg grins between us.

I'm teetering on a high, I can't contain myself. I feel as if happiness is exuding from my pores, making me glow. We're at Tap 42, central hangout in the yachtie world of Fort Lauderdale. A constellation of wire bulbs stab down at us from the ceiling, casting our faces in an orangey golden light. Greg looks like he's died and gone to heaven as we strain to hear each other over the hubbub.

"I can't believe it. Monaco? The Med?" Cailee rests her chin on a fist. "My little Aurora. All growed up."

"So he just came right back out?" Greg says, shaking his head. "Like, a minute later?"

"I know, right? And that picture he took. *Weird*."

"Don't forget the creepy receptionist chilling in the dark," Greg adds.

A thought has occurred to Cailee, though. She asks, cutting through all this, "What was the yacht called again?"

I smirk around the rim of my beer. "The *Lair*."

But the look Cailee and Greg give each other makes my face slacken.

"What?"

Greg fails spectacularly at an indifferent shrug. "Nothing. Just . . . it's owned by Adrian Voper. The reclusive billionaire."

"And he's supposed to be *hot*," Cailee chimes in.

"Yeah?" I say with a strange coiling in my gut. "What does he look like?"

"That's just it," Greg says. "No one knows. Nobody's ever gotten a picture of him."

My turn to shrug. "Aren't all those yacht owners super private?"

"Sure," Greg concedes. "But this one's also a nightmare to work for. Like, OCD, a super control freak—"

"I think that's all she needs to hear, don't you?" Cailee says lightly, and Greg flushes.

"Yeah, sure. Of course." He takes a swig from his beer, looks at it. "Another round?"

"With haste, sir!" Cailee cries. "I am in grieving!"

Greg gives me a look—*Good luck*—and sidles off for the bar. A grin tugs at my lips as I watch him go. "He's not so bad, you know."

Cailee glances over her shoulder. "Yeah, I know."

I watch my best friend. Once, I would have been beyond excited at all this. Going out, bars, being on our own. The buoyant thrill of possibility, of knowing anything could happen. Anybody could happen. But that was gone now. No dancing for me. No flirting. Not after what happened.

Not after Josh.

Cailee turns to me with glassy eyes, and that's when I know it's coming. I beat her to it. "Cailee. Honey."

Her lips pout. "But what am I gonna do *without you?*" she wails, dramatically flinging her head back, and I feel my eyes sting and open my arms. "Oh, babe, c'mere."

She walks into them, plopping her chin on my shoulder like a lost puppy. "You better call me. Like, all the time."

"I will." I stroke her hair.

"And get me hired on the same boat once you've seduced the owner."

"Of course."

She sniffles. "Okay."

"Okay."

When she draws back, her cheeks are shining. I wipe at them. "You gonna hook up with Greg tonight?"

Her face screws up as she thinks about it. "Yeah. Probably."

I snort. "Good ole Cailee."

"Damn right." She pauses, assessing me. "You're still not gonna party with me, are you?"

I shake my head.

She nods, and we look into each other's eyes. She's suddenly very solemn. "Don't worry. The right guy will come around. You just need time."

I have to swallow the lump in my throat before I respond. "I know."

We're holding each other like prom dates by the time Greg comes back.

THREE

It's a twelve-hour flight from Fort Lauderdale to Nice.

I've never flown before. I grip the armrests of my seat like a child as we rumble into the sky, my heart hammering against my sternum. I only open my eyes once we've reached cruising altitude. All around me, fliers look bored, staring out windows or scrolling through movie selections. Of course they'd be calm. They'd have no reason to feel like a fugitive.

I didn't feel this way when I drove with Cailee across the US and saw the sign for the Sunshine State flash by. With Cailee, I could pretend that Florida was merely a girls' trip, a mad interlude that would soon end and bring me back home. Back to Josh.

But this—this is final. There's no going back from this.

This is real.

Absurdly, infuriatingly, I feel like I'm betraying him. As if, deep down, there is something wrong with the world.

This is what he's taught me. To need his approval so badly that the very idea of disagreeing with him, let alone defying and leaving him, makes me physically sick, my insides twisting into knots.

A sudden, wrenching agitation overtakes me. I'm trapped here. I have to escape. I have to sleep. I fumble out melatonin pills and knock them back, expecting my adrenaline and chronic insomnia to keep me up. But I crash at once.

I dream of Josh, as I always do. I see our beginning when he lavished me with attention. Him taking me into his garage hung with old Nirvana posters where he plays guitar for me, making me feel like he's led me into his secret world. A place of enchantment where I trust him completely, where I am so addicted to his love that I will do anything, endure anything, to get it. Then the dreams come in jagged flashes as the dark Josh who had always been lying in wait comes out. I see him questioning where I was, demanding to see my phone. I see his dark, judging looks, his contemptuous smirk. As if he's grown weary of me, or my devotion disgusts him, perhaps scares him. I see him pushing me away, almost as if in anticipation of my eventually abandoning him. As a way to make me prove my love to him. To absolve himself of his behavior by projecting it onto me. I see him twisting my words until the tears are gathering plump and trembling at the corners of my eyes. I see the noise and chaos, shouting and things breaking. I see him punching a wall by my head and leaving me to slide down it and hug my knees, my eyes as blank as stones.

I see the other things that I do not want to see.

When I wake, chest heaving and eyes flying to make sure he's not here, he's not on the plane, the mom next to me says, "You okay, hon?"

Something hot and nasty surges up the back of my throat. I grope past her and into the lavatory, suck in a huge lungful of air and put my hands to my mouth, holding in a wracking sob.

Even here, even thirty-six thousand feet in the air and halfway across the world, I can't escape him.

Maybe he was right. Maybe I'll always be his.

Because, in the end, that was the heart of it: He was afraid of love because he did not believe he was deserving of it. So he had to destroy you, too, so you felt you didn't deserve more than the twisted illusion he had to offer you.

In the aisle outside, I hear a chime go off. Flight attendants bustle by. There's an announcement over the speakers. We're landing in France.

By the time I leave the hotel the next morning, I'm myself again. I've done my daily yoga session, which always clears my head, and the wonder is starting to set in. I've never been outside of the US before—hell, before Florida I'd never been outside of Oregon—and I'm fluttery with nerves as the train snakes along the coast of France. I'm trying to calm my breathing by the time it glides into the twinkly, cavernous station at Monte Carlo and I disembark with my roller bag behind me, eyes wide. I'm inside a hollowed-out mountain, and commuters stream toward a huge jagged cleft in it—the exit. My heart clenches in my chest. I follow and emerge blinking onto a cobbled street lined with brightly colored stucco houses—pink, yellow, cream—with the salty clean smell of the sea in my nostrils. Ahead, tourists crowd a rail, pointing and gawking. I shoulder my way through and understand why.

The world falls away. Against the face of the mountain, cobbled streets switchback down, and down, and down for miles in a dizzying, dynamic landscape to the Monaco Grand Prix racetrack. And beyond, a fleet of gleaming white yachts—the jewels of the French Riviera—nestled in rows in Port Hercule, helicopters hovering about them like dragonflies. And beyond that, the sea.

It's the most breathtakingly beautiful thing I've ever seen.

It seems to take forever for me to descend via elevator down through the mountain and emerge at sea level, my roller bag bumping and bouncing behind me down the cobbled streets. Men whistle and catcall in French and English as I pass in my yachtie skirt and polo, and I ignore them, double-checking the rendezvous point.

The yachts stretch on and on, endless. One gleaming monstrosity after another. Their crews nod to me as I go.

Then I stop at an empty spot, frowning. Why here?

A low drone, and I see a gleaming limousine tender gliding toward me across the light blue waves. It slows and a man in a white polo and khaki shorts calls out from the foredeck. "Miss Strand?"

"Uh, yeah?" God, why can't I be smooth?

"I'm Jason. First mate of the *Lair*." He holds out a hand, a coiling red dragon flexing across the bulky curve of his bicep. "I'll take that for you."

So. The first mate's a tatted hunk.

I pass him my bag, and then—white teeth showing in a perfect smile—he offers his hand again. I take it, blushing, and step lightly down onto the boat. The young deckhand behind the wheel waits until we're seated in the stern before speeding the tender away in a long, smooth arc back out to sea.

The tumbling in my gut and light spray on my face is both terrifying and exhilarating.

Jason watches me knowingly. "First time for everything, right?"

"You could say that," I laugh, and glance back at the receding armada of yachts. "Sooo, where's the *Lair*?"

Jason's mouth tugs in a rakish grin. "At the moment, Port Hercule doesn't have a berth big enough for her." He turns and points. "So, we made do."

I follow his gaze, and gape.

The *Lair* is not merely big—it's enormous. All on its lonesome at the far right of the bay, it's easily the biggest yacht in the harbor by a third—at least a hundred and thirty meters from stem to stern. As we near, skimming the waves in its shadow, my eyes can barely comprehend its immensity: a floating paradise of

Jacuzzis and pools and sweeping staircases. As sharp and dazzling as a kitchen knife, with an extended bow and curving floor-to-ceiling walls of glass, it looks like some glowering submarine straight out of *20,000 Leagues Under the Sea*. Banter floats through the air, and I realize deckhands are hanging off its sides in harnesses to hose it down to an immaculate sheen.

Is this even real?

We round the stern, and now I can see the gleaming transom emblazoned with LAIR in huge stainless-steel letters. As the tender's engine is killed and we coast lazily toward the swim deck, I spot a woman standing on the aft main deck waiting for us. She's in an elegant black skirt and blindingly white button-down, hands clasped before her as she watches us arrive. Her blonde hair is pinned severely back in an updo that reminds me of the tragic blondes in those old Hitchcock movies, though this blonde looks Asian—Chinese, perhaps—and I realize she's the first person of color I've seen in the yachting industry. The distinction appears to have been hard-won—she has the pinched look of someone who never smiles.

Her low voice floats toward us. "You must be Miss Strand."

A noticeable but polished accent there. What lingers though is the cool reserve in that voice—the control.

It's chilling.

Jason is already escorting me onto the foredeck of the tender. He hops onto the *Lair*'s swim deck and I follow, his arms waiting for me. I look up as my bag is placed at my feet. "Hello. I hope I'm not late."

The woman presses her lips together, as if suppressing the urge to say I am, and sniffs in through her narrow nose. "I am Mrs. Colding, the Chief Stewardess. I'll show you the boat, and then we'll get you to work." Her eyes slide to Jason. "Mr. Young. I believe we are no longer in need of your services."

Jason flicks an amused look at me, and I smile. "Thank you." He hangs his head in a bow—mocking or genuine, I can't tell which. "Miss Strand." Then he bounds up the stairs onto the main deck—a brief glance passes between him and Mrs. Colding—and he's gone.

Mrs. Colding returns her imperious gaze to me. "Ready?"

I swallow and nod. *Let's hope so.*

FOUR

"The *Lair* is seven decks tall. This is the lower deck."

Mrs. Colding sweeps a hand toward the interior, and I gape. A beach club complete with cocktail bar stretches before me, its key element a pool stretching for nearly the length of the deck, Jacuzzis at the back and lounging areas on either side—all sprinkled about with rose petals. "An internal seawater pool," Mrs. Colding explains. "Mr. Voper spends a lot of his time here." She points to retractable glass panels inset into the main deck above, a darkly tinted window to the sky. "He likes to open these up at night." She picks up an iPad and taps it, and I jump as a portion of the yacht's hull folds out with a hydraulic whir to turn into an extended patio for the lounge area. Sunlight sweeps in. "These and the roof are *never* to be opened unless personally requested by myself or Mr. Voper. Understood?"

I nod, wondering if my farm girl awe is showing yet—*Where am I right now?*—and straighten my spine. She doesn't need to know I'm from Bumfudge, Nowhere.

Mrs. Colding taps the iPad again and sets it down. "This way."

We pass beyond the lower deck's beach club and down a side passageway. A series of glass doors here. "Spa. Sauna room." She opens the last door. "And snow room."

Snow room? Are you kidding me? I peek my head in and there, yes, beyond a second, huge wooden door Mrs. Colding has hauled wide, is snow: a small grotto of winter, drifts of fluffy white snowflakes clinging to the artfully jagged slabs of stone composing the floor and walls. Even icicles hang from the ceiling, like some glittering cave in Lapland. My breath fogs in the air and I hug myself and back away. "Wow."

"Another of Mr. Voper's favorites. This will have to be ready at all times. Understood?"

I sharply nod. "Got it."

Mrs. Colding shuts the door. "Next deck."

On the main deck, lounging areas surround the glass panels that were the lower deck's pool roof. A sickly sweetness hits me, and I see it: an overwhelming display of Grand Prix red roses guiding me to a pair of glass double doors. It's a fantasia, a floral fairy tale. Smartly dressed stewardesses pass to and fro bearing vases, and Mrs. Colding looks over her shoulder at me as she opens the double doors. "A Voper standard. They're flown in fresh every week." I'm unable to form a reply, for we've entered a spacious dining room that all but stops my heart. It's filled with banquet tables with rose centerpieces, an immense chandelier hanging through the deck above via a circular hole ringed by a flaring of ornately carved metal suffused with mood lighting. Sweeping staircases flank the far wall and all is surrounded by floor-to-ceiling glass. I try to gather my breath. "The windows," I say, and Mrs. Colding turns to me. "They're all tinted."

Mrs. Colding holds herself with witchy stillness, eyes like dark stones. "Mr. Voper prefers it that way," she says with chilling finality, and sweeps away.

Okayyy . . . so questions not welcomed. Got it.

"Notice the hidden staircases behind the main ones," Mrs. Colding points out. "That is for the stewardesses when serving, as we must do our best to never get underfoot. Yes?"

"Yes, ma'am."

"Good."

She passes both for a passageway leading beyond the dining room, opens a door onto a lavish cabin with a huge fuckdoll bed and stone shower. Seriously? And—surprise, surprise—more roses. "There are twelve staterooms on the deck above," Mrs. Colding says, "but these are the two VIP suites and the ones you will be maintaining on this trip." She picks up an iPad and gestures at an outline in the wall. "Again, you must have permission to open the foldable platforms."

She strides on, and we come to a sort of antechamber before a pair of imposing double doors stained a deep red. "This," she announces, "is Mr. Voper's suite. I am the only one who cleans it. No one else can enter. This is the most important rule aboard this boat." Mrs. Colding's eyes bore into me. "Is that clear?"

I feel a prickling chill go down my spine. "Yes, ma'am."

The eyes stare on, unblinking. Then she sweeps away. "Next deck."

It all begins to blur at this point. An entertainment lounge, its glittering chandelier the one hanging through into the dining room below. Another bar, its top a thick slab of black marble veined with color. Stateroom after stateroom. On the top deck another Jacuzzi surrounded by lounging pads for sunbathing. A fully stocked wet bar. On the sun deck a supersized bathtub and more sun lounges. I've never seen such extravagance in my life. I don't even know what planet I'm on anymore.

And everywhere, on every deck, those pervasive roses, their heavy scent sweetening the air.

At some point we come across a library and my heart leaps. It's packed with books with ancient spines, globes and portraits and a baby grand piano. Now *this* is how I'd spend my money . . .

"Another Voper favorite. You must always knock before entering." Mrs. Colding faces me. "That's the basic tour. You will discover more rooms the longer you're aboard." As I grapple with that thought, she looks me up and down with merciless coldness. "Do you know what a stewardess' job entails?"

I open my mouth. "I—"

"Never mind, I am not interested in your conception of a stewardess' responsibilities. This is what's to be expected aboard this boat. You are fourth stew, which means you are the least qualified and the most in need to prove yourself. You will rotate schedules with the other stews to share service, housekeeping and laundry, but you will not serve meals until I am satisfied with your silver service. You will wake up at six a.m. every morning without exception, and you will not retire without my say-so. Every moment of every day, the only thought in your head will be service. If you see a guest touch a light switch, you will wipe the fingerprint from that light switch. If you see them use the bathroom sink, you will wipe that sink spotless the moment they leave. You will obey their every whim—nothing is forbidden to them. And this goes most especially for Mr. Voper. You should know that his standards are not the same as ours. He requires perfection, and so I have been trained to give him that. Do not interfere with his routine. Do not burden him with mistakes, because he will not stand for them. Do not drop drinks or stumble in front of guests. Do not speak unless spoken to. Do not bother, pester, annoy, or flirt. You are merely there to anticipate his every need. You are both essential and absolutely nothing. You will look as he likes, curtsy as he likes, breathe as he likes. And if you compromise the service aboard this boat in any way, I will strand you on the first beach I see. Now." And for the first time, horrifyingly, Mrs. Colding's mouth widens in a smile. "Is that all clear to you, Miss Strand?"

"Y-Yes," I manage, shrinking into myself.

"Excellent." Mrs. Colding unclips a crew radio from her hip and simpers into it. "Miss Digby, could you meet us in the library, please?"

"Right away, Mrs. Colding," a voice crackles back.

Mrs. Colding and I stare at each other, and in what seems like the blink of an eye we're joined by a fiercely cute girl my age, blonde hair in a ponytail and a bit out of breath. "Yes, Mrs. Colding?"

Mrs. Colding's eyes never leave me. "Miss Digby. Could you show Miss Strand here the cabin you'll be sharing so she can change into her new uniform?" And those black eyes crinkle mirthlessly. "Miss Strand is ready to work."

FIVE

I follow in a daze through a sparkling galley, past rows of meat lockers and down a winding staircase to a tiny, underlit cabin with a bunkbed and a shower that looks smaller than a broom closet. So, this is where the slaves are kept.

The stewardess is eyeing me with a grin. "Got it full-bore from the old witch, huh?"

"Jesus, I thought I was gonna throw up," I say, and my new bunkmate laughs. "What happened? Someone strangle her lover and dump him overboard?"

"Search me," says my bunkmate, lips quirked. "The bets are still going. I've been first stew on the *Lair* for three years now and I still don't have a clue. But don't worry—you'll do fine." She holds out a hand. "I'm Dorothea, by the way. But you can call me Thea."

"Aurora. But you can call me Arie."

We grin at each other.

"So. What'd you think of Jason?"

Once in my new black skirt and short-sleeved white

dress shirt, a crew radio clipped to my hip, I begin detailing the VIP suites with Thea. We come prepared, bringing cleaning caddies stocked to the brim with glass cleaner, bath cleaner, toilet bowl cleaner, Formula 409, diluted Murphy's Oil Soap, scrub brushes, sponges, leather chamois, feather dusters, Q-tips. I'm wearing yellow latex gloves and scrubbing grout out of floor tiles with a toothbrush when Thea begins laughing. "This what you thought you were getting yourself into?" she snorts.

"Har har," I say, and we both grin. "So, what's the deal with Voper and Mrs. Colding? Only her cleaning his cabin . . .?"

Thea shrugs. "It's always been like that."

"She in love with him or something?"

Thea barks a laugh. "Now that's an idea."

"Old spinster."

Thea makes an equivocating noise. "Think what you want, but Mrs. Colding is unmarried because nobody is good enough for Mrs. Colding. She'll probably live happily ever after by herself."

I think on that one. "And where's Mr. Voper hiding? He only come out at night or something?"

Thea scrubs with her own toothbrush around the toilet. "Oh, he's not here yet. Picking up some playthings on the mainland. He'll probably arrive later tonight—he likes to make an entrance." Her toothbrush slows, and I frown at her.

"That bad, huh?"

She shrugs. "I'd . . . be careful."

I sit back and arm the sweat from my brow. "What's he like?"

Thea sits back, too. "He's . . . *particular.*"

"As in?"

She looks at me. "As in, be what he wants you to be."

Hours pass. Light leaches away into a brooding dusk of cool blues—and still no word on Voper's arrival. When I travel from the main deck to the bridge deck, lugging my caddy, the deckhands are prowling about in their epauletted dress whites, idly wiping at the railings with their chamois and fluffing deck pillows. The yacht is spotless.

Such stillness. The lights of Monte Carlo have begun to wink on, preparing for night, a glowing, golden constellation set back amongst the hills. As if in answer, the *Lair*'s exterior lighting systems pulse on, and I look over the side to see a deep, lurid red radiating from every deck and into the water around the hull, lighting up the dark harbor with a bloody fire.

She's ready.

My crew radio whines at my hip. "Owner is arriving. Five minutes."

Utter chaos. A crush of bodies pound down the gangways, and Thea suddenly grabs my arm. "Come on."

We follow to the bow, where a crew of what must be forty people stand in a half-circle before a lit-up helipad. Thea pushes me into a gap at the end of the stews and I look about. Everyone is here. Mrs. Colding, Captain

Redfearn in a black captain's coat. Jason gives me a wink and I smile back.

Beside me, the second and third stews are giving me a look. "What?" I say, and they exchange glances.

"No one's told you to bleach your hair yet?"

And that's when I realize: All the stews are blonde. My hand instinctively goes up to my coal-black hair. "N-No. Why?"

The third stew smirks. "Mr. Voper? Guy's a freak. Gives us all a hundred extra bucks a month so we can get our hair maintained. I'm a redhead." She side-eyes me. "Good luck, brunette."

I swallow and look over at Mrs. Colding, who's already watching me with lips pursed in withering disdain. *Did she set me up?*

And that's when everyone falls silent—for a distant whumping can be heard.

It's the rotors of a helicopter. A faint light can be seen, a dark object gliding over the sea. The crew stand at stiff attention, in perfect symmetry. They know what's expected.

The whumping soon becomes a roar, and before I know it a gleaming black shape descends out of the darkness in a hurricane of noise and alights on the helipad. My eyes instantly water and I try to stand erect as the blur of rotors threatens to knock me on my ass. Wouldn't that be a great first impression.

A door swings open and a long female leg glides out. A gorgeous rucked dress, the neckline diving almost to the midriff. Then familiar puffy lips, a sleek sheet of blonde hair—Emmie Gallagher.

My jaw drops.

Another supermodel in a chic black dress descends, and then Italian leather shoes, a dark suit probably handmade by some European atelier. And then I see him, one arm around each of these two tall, glittering creatures with the easy hauteur of a king: Mr. Voper. His skin is unusually pale for a yacht owner, the clean bulk of his jaw tight and muscled from constant, irritated clenching, his lips full and lush. His hair is a slick-looking, contained black bramble. But the eyes I've been so dreading to judge me are hidden behind black designer glasses.

As the rotor blades wind down, I find I've been holding my breath.

"Mr. Voper," Captain Redfearn says, tipping his hat. "Welcome aboard."

"Arnold," Mr. Voper grits, those cruel, lush lips pressed together as the glasses sweep the assembled crew. I shiver. "Ready to depart?"

"At your word, sir." Even in the captain's voice, there is the slightest tremble of fear. "I was thinking—"

But Mr. Voper lifts a hand; he's staring at a nearby deckhand. "What is this?" he says with lethal quiet.

The air chills. The deckhand, a fresh-faced Australian lad, looks down at his shirt. One corner is untucked.

He pales. "Sorry, sir. I was in a hurry and—"

"Get off my boat."

The order rings in the air with appalling clarity. The deckhand's mouth hangs. He flies a look at the captain, but finds no help there. His teeth click together and he eels his way out of the lineup, head hung and ears red.

I find my heart is thudding in my chest.

When the deckhand's gone, Mr. Voper lets out a cleansing "So." He lifts his brows at the two women on his arms. "How does Corsica sound?"

They glance at each other, lips curled in smug smirks. "It'll do."

Mr. Voper turns to the captain. "It seems the vote is in."

Another tip of the hat. "Right away, sir." Captain Redfearn gestures, and the deck crew scurry to their positions, seamless as smoke. Mr. Voper strides on.

"Your staterooms are ready. Cocktails first, perhaps? The top deck?" Mrs. Colding has fallen in step with them like an old confidante.

Mr. Voper nods. "Always on point, Mrs. Colding."

"Have you eaten? Supper can be ready in minutes."

"A snack for the ladies, perhaps."

Emmie flips her hair. "Just some escargot for me. You do have that, don't you?"

Mrs. Colding's face is inscrutable. "Of course. Right away."

They're heading right for me. I hold my breath, willing them to pass by, for Mr. Voper to not notice—

No such luck: the glasses turn, the entourage stops.

Absolute silence. You could count the waves lapping against the hull. Emmie and the other model glance at each other, confused.

Then Mr. Voper lifts a hand, snicks his glasses away, and our eyes meet.

For a moment I am lost in the burning centroids of anger that are those eyes—the intensity, the eerie blue power of them—and I feel the world quiver.

Never have eyes like that looked on me.

One long, pale hand lifts—his hands are almost like a woman's—and feels the rich darkness of my ponytail coiled on my shoulder. Vertigo takes me. "I—I'm sorry," I splutter. "I forgot to bleach—"

But like that, he's moved on—a tall, lean presence gliding past. Emmie gives me a smirk over her shoulder, and I cannot even begin to interpret the blank expression on Mrs. Colding's face.

All I know is, the totality of me has been summed up—and dismissed.

SIX

We get them set up on the top deck with gin and tonics, a platter of escargot and a charcuterie board. Emmie and the other girl, a Spanish swimwear model—Lucia, I think?—flounce giggling in bikinis into the bubbling Jacuzzi, the shimmying moons of their asses bouncing. Mr. Voper doesn't join them. He looms with hands in pockets at the edge, dark hair glossy from the Jacuzzi's glowing light, as the models feed each other nibbles of cheese and give him sultry looks.

Dear God, I think, wanting to roll my eyes.

"Anything else, sir?" I offer as casually as I can, and Mrs. Colding shoots me a sharp look. That was her line, apparently.

But I hold my ground, heart pounding, waiting for an answer.

It seems to take forever. Mr. Voper turns his head slightly to me—then raises a distracted hand, as if warding off a fly.

Oh.

"Aren't you coming in?" Emmie purrs, plump lips sucking suggestively on a wedge of Stilton, and Lucia cozies up to her and gives Adrian a seductive onceover. "We're getting lonely, *papi.*"

Mr. Voper's mouth twitches. He half turns. "That'll be all for now, Mrs. Colding."

"Of course, sir," Mrs. Colding says, bowing, and tugs at my arm. Her fingers are like a vise. When I glance back, Mr. Voper is loosening his tie as Emmie and Lucia watch with undisguised hunger.

On the sun deck, Mrs. Colding turns to me and hisses through gritted teeth. "*Never* do that again. The Chief Stewardess always leads. Understand?"

I nod. I'm trembling from head to foot, I don't know why. I blurt it out before I can stop myself. "Do you have any hair bleach?" Mrs. Colding blinks at me like a toad and I add, "My hair." I gesture helplessly. "All the other stews . . ."

Mrs. Colding takes in a long, slow breath and says in a careful tone, "If he hasn't told you to bleach your hair, then don't."

I stare at her. "But—he *hates* me."

Mrs. Colding gives me a flat look. "That's why he's paying you, darling. So he can hate someone."

I swallow, letting this sink in, and try to get my trembling under control. Mrs. Colding surveys me coolly, head to toe. "You should turn in. You have a long day tomorrow."

"Yes, Mrs. Colding."

Ten minutes of confused wandering later, I find my cabin and roll into my bunk, pulling the sheets up to my chin. I think of calling Cailee, but I can't. I don't know what I'm feeling.

The alarm on my phone goes off at some ungodly hour and I hit snooze twice before I remember what and where I am. A stewardess. On a superyacht in the Mediterranean. Who needs to get up at six a.m. *Shit.* I hop up to see Thea is already gone. I hastily wash my face, throw on some makeup and run upstairs. The chef has a quick breakfast waiting for me, and then it's on to "heads and beds"—cleaning the staterooms. I'm on housekeeping duty today, and the guests are already up.

While the other stews serve breakfast on the bridge deck, I grab a cleaning caddy and get to work. Emmie's room is a mess. Lacy panties on the floor, a bottle of lube on the bed, rose petals and anal beads among the rumpled sheets . . .

My face is hot, I suddenly can't look anywhere long. What is wrong with me? *Get it together, Aurora.*

After making the bed, corners hospital perfect, I notice the Louis Vuitton luggage in the walk-in wardrobe—and a pair of diamond-encrusted Stuart Weitzman pumps. My jaw hangs. It wasn't only two weeks ago that I was drooling over the same pair in a fashion magazine, knowing I'd never be able to have them. They cost more than I make in a month.

I glance at the door, biting my lip—and chicken out.

Professional, Aurora. Be a goddamn professional.

I'm gathering up fallen clothes worth a small fortune when I hear footsteps. I whirl, heart in throat—and Emmie Gallagher all but runs into me. "Oh, hello," she says, taking a step back.

I'm all hot in the face again. "Excuse me, I—I'll get out of your way—"

"You're fine, keep doing your thing," Emmie trills with a little toss of her wrist and disappears into the wardrobe. I'm frozen with indecision. Clothes still in my arms, I lean to the side and catch a glimpse of bare flesh, a sexy, Parisian-looking swimsuit getting thrown on. Why can't I have legs like that?

This is what I have always done: envied other women's bodies—compared my body to other women's bodies—because Josh never seemed to take any interest in mine.

But isn't that what all women do?

When Emmie sallies out again, I pluck up the nerve. "I don't know if you remember me—Aurora, from high school?"

She looks me up and down, lash extensions fluttering. Then holds up a crop top. "I'll need this stain out by tonight." She adds it to the pile in my arms and saunters out, nose in the air.

It takes me a moment to register it, for the indignant rage to come.

What. A. *Bitch.*

I look over at the Stuart Weitzman pumps in the wardrobe, and my lip snarls. *Screw it. I'm probably getting kicked off this boat, anyway.* I drop the clothes, kick off my cheap Sperry deck shoes and jam my bare feet into the pumps, Cinderella reverence be damned. My heart is pounding, sweat beading my forehead. I don't care. I'm drunk on disobedience, the sick, exquisite thrill of it. I'm so angry it takes a full minute before I realize the pumps are a perfect fit. I turn my ankle, admiring the sparkle of diamonds. I prance back and forth before the mirror, taking myself in. I'm exultant. I've never felt so adult, so glamorous. I envision myself on a runway. A man's arm. Voper's arm. Cameras are flashing, I'm radiant and full of significance. I am seen. I am—

Emmie Gallagher stands behind me, a delicious smirk on her face.

I let out a little shriek and stumble, grabbing onto the clothesline. In a flash the pumps are off and I'm smoothing down my skirt, hands fluttering. I can't breathe. "Is there anything I can do for you?" I manage, not quite meeting her eyes.

It's a game. An understanding between us. I pretend I wasn't snooping, and she pretends she didn't see me. She knows the rules instantly. She's a woman, after all.

"Just forgot my hat," she says with poisonous innocence, and I turn and see a big floppy sunhat on a shelf. I hand it to her. A subtle look, a lift of one finely plucked eyebrow, and she's gone.

I clutch at the shelves, destroyed.

How's the rest of this charter gonna go *now?*

SEVEN

By the time I've finished cleaning the cabins and main areas, it's time to join Mrs. Colding for guest watch. Anxiety prickles through me. Tucking in my shirt and patting at my hair, I follow the shrieks of laughter to the stern and find we're in no port.

All around me, needles of rock slant out of the clearest turquoise waters I've ever seen. We're floating in a collection of low islets, the sun a warm, flaring delirium overhead, a snapshot of paradise. Beyond: the low, verdant cliffs of Corsica. As I descend one of the grand staircases flanking the swim deck, Emmie and Lucia jump shrieking and giggling into the water, tanned skin gleaming as they bob like mermaids and call out. "Come on, baby! Come join us!"

That's when I see Mr. Voper lurking in the dark mouth of the tender garage, hands in pockets, Mrs. Colding at his elbow. He shakes his head and the girls poopoo him. "Oh, come on!" they cry, but he doesn't move. They make pouty faces.

Mr. Voper's mouth twitches in amusement. "How about Jason takes you out on the water for a while?"

Jason and another deckhand are drifting up on Jet Skis, grinning. "We'll have a snack and some fun inside later."

This seems to mollify the models. They look at each other and smirk. "Okay." They climb up behind Jason and the deckhand, and Emmie makes an admiring sound as she holds on to Jason's muscular frame. He grins at her over his shoulder and they speed away in a flume of spray.

I turn, heart pounding, to greet Mr. Voper. Even on holiday, he hasn't changed into more casual clothes, nothing to indicate he's in the sun-loving Mediterranean. He's buttoned up in a dark fitted suit like a priest or mortician: cool, urbane, closed off. His sunglasses glide to me, and I feel sparks and chills sweep me head to toe. *Jesus, am I that terrified of him?* The moment comes, I open my mouth to speak—

Mrs. Colding steps between, her mouth a grim line. "Stay here and wait for them." And she follows Voper into the yacht.

I stand there, stuck with a vague feeling of rejection. How ridiculous. I snap myself out of it and go stand on one of the foldable platforms extending like a balcony out from the yacht, hands clasped behind my back. Far off, the Jet Skis thunder across the water, followed faintly by Emmie and Lucia's squeals of delight. I crane my head and look down the length of the yacht. Sunlight flares off its polished exterior, but I can see Voper pacing behind the darkly tinted windows of the main salon like a hungry shadow, watching the models, too. It must be lonely, being rich. Lonely and alienating, imprisoned in your own wealth. Though he has Mrs. Colding there at his elbow, with her baleful looks and her inscrutable, fanatical loyalty. What is it with the two of them? What strange relationship do they have?

It's almost half an hour before the guests return. Emmie is giggling and pushing at Jason, and they both tumble laughing into the water. I grit my teeth. And when Emmie climbs voluptuously up the swim ladder as if vamping for a magazine shoot, she flicks her hair back in an arc of sparkling water droplets and struts over to take my offered towel, her expression suddenly contemptuous. "Water," she says without any inflection at all.

My teeth are outright grinding now.

When I open the cooler in the beach club, I'm at a loss at the number of brands: Evian, Voss, Fiji, Acqua Pana. I've no idea which one Emmie takes, but I can't admit that. So I go for the most expensive. Evian it is.

When I hand it to her, she looks me up and down—and grabs it, breaking the seal with a brutal twist. She jerks her head at a dripping Lucia. "You gonna get her one, too? Or did you wanna try her shoes on first?"

I flush a deep red. Lucia puts her hands on her hips, shares a smirk with Emmie.

So. This is how it's gonna go.

Great.

As I turn back for the water cooler, Lucia mutters loud enough for me to hear, "And I thought the peasants in my country were bad." Emmie snorts water as Lucia calls after me. "You think if you were tall enough to walk a runway, you'd be in one of the VIP suites with us? Those shoes won't make that shit any prettier, *querida.*"

My blood is boiling now. *Why can't I stand up for myself?* I look over my shoulder at Jason, who's removing his water jacket behind them, and he rolls his eyes. I can't help but grin. Maybe it'll be bearable after all.

It's just enough of a boost in confidence for me to mutter under my breath, "Too bad *your* prettiness is only skin-deep."

There's an astonished silence behind me.

"*What* did you say?"

Shit.

Blood thuds behind my eyes. When I turn around, the mouths of the models are hanging open in gobsmacked fury. Jason has to turn away to hide his grin.

I fight down a prickling of shock, my hands trembling at my sides—*What did I just do?*—and plaster an oh-so-innocent smile on my face. "I said, Which kind of water did you want, miss?"

When I glance up at the salon windows again, Voper is watching me.

We anchor near Ajaccio for the night. I do cabin turn-downs, help Mrs. Colding and Thea clear dinner—Voper never even looks at me—and after some laundry I'm let go for the night. I barely notice; I'm still a little in wonder at what I'd said. That I'd had the balls to say it, mutter though it was. And my lie had hardly fooled Emmie and Lucia—they'd glared at me all night.

Too bad I'll never have the confidence to say something like that to their faces.

When I shamble like the undead into the cabin, Thea is still up. "Well?" she says, hanging her head off the side of the top bunk as I sink into mine. "How was your first full day?"

I heave a sigh, and Thea arches a brow. When I tell her about the shoes she rolls away, throwing her head back in delighted laughter and clapping her hands together. "You didn't. You *didn't!* Oh my God, you're *so* screwed."

I lay a forearm across my eyes and groan.

"You've got issues, girl." She's still cracking up.

"Tell me about it. I kinda gave her and Lucia some lip today, too." I pause. "And then there's Voper . . ."

Thea is still with curiosity above me. "What about him?"

I glance at my cell. I've got no less than twelve texts from Cailee. The last one reads: *ARE YOU DEAD?? CALL ME!!!* Time to spare her the agony.

I hop out of my bunk. "I gotta make a call."

Thea rolls on her side. "Good luck with that."

"Any recommendations?"

She frowns. "Try the stern. It's usually the most private at this time."

I flash a grin at her. "Thanks."

The yacht has an odd calm to it at night, an eerie, drifting feeling, like a vast dreaming presence. Its lurid red lighting system suffuses the waters about it with a wavering glow. I tiptoe down the teak gangway of the main deck in my bare feet, cell phone gripped tight, feeling like an impostor. I've almost stumbled through the hole before I realize the huge retractable panels of the pool roof are open.

I freeze, the blood drumming in my ears at the import of this. I know I should turn away, but I can't. I inch to the edge and peek down.

Not twenty feet below, a body floats in the yacht's lit-up internal pool, like a corpse at a crime scene.

It's Voper.

This is when I should *really* turn away, I know, retire from my short career as a voyeur and go back to bed. I have stumbled on something that is private, intimate; something that should not be seen. But I can't. I can't turn away—my curiosity is too strong. It is impossible. I have to look on, like some figure in a fairy tale. I am enchanted. My eyes travel over his face, tracing its softness and hard angles. He looks strangely vulnerable, innocent, in this moment. Those full lips are blue, cold and bloodless. His eyes shut, lashes dark and curved against his cheeks, like a child's.

The eyes suddenly fly open—staring right at me.

I jerk away, body tensed and hyperventilating. *Fuck. Fuckity-fuck-fuck.* What do I do? I'm about to make a break for it when a mild voice drifts up out of the opening, rooting me to the spot. "Come on down. Don't be shy."

Nice knowing you, Aurora.

EIGHT

There's no going back now. I find the staircase leading down into the beach club and emerge into a space aglow with pool-lights casting wavering reflections on the walls. It's as if I'm in the inward parts of some leviathan.

Voper has his back to me, elbows propped on the pool edge, hair slicked with water. Waiting.

I find I'm shivering.

What am I doing here? I part my lips. My voice comes out steadier than expected. "Can I help you, sir?"

His head turns slightly. His voice is a little wondering. "Help me." He snorts, not unkindly. Then looks ahead again. "Are you going to come closer?"

I swallow, knees trembling, and slowly round the pool. His body floats pale and luminous as a fish before him, too blurred by the water to be seen clearly. His voice is hard with curiosity. "What are you doing wandering about at this hour?"

My heart thumps against my ribcage. I hold up my cell phone. "Just—calling a friend."

A long moment before he nods, smooth brow furrowing, as if this is a new phenomenon to him. "Ah," he says softly. "Yes." He appears to feel no pressure to fill the following silence.

I do.

"Your supermodel friends must be looking for you." I offer it up as a joke, but the faint smile that creases his face lets me know it amuses him in some other way.

"Yes," he says, with something like sadness. "I suppose they must be." Then his voice changes, glinting with something new. "Or perhaps they're still smarting from your comment today."

Heat rushes into my face. The words trip out of my mouth. "I shouldn't have said that—"

"Or perhaps someone should have said it to them a long time ago."

The remark leaves my head spinning. *Did he just say that?*

"It's very rare that I'm amused," he goes on. "I must thank you for that. I've never seen a model break so much Christofle crystal in one night."

I stand there, my heart hammering. I don't know what to make of his attitude. He won't even look at me, but there's an accessibility here that's not been present before. It's like a tender bruise; I have to touch it.

"Why . . ." I say, but trail off. Mrs. Colding would execute me.

That's when Voper looks at me, and the shock of it urges me on.

"Why don't you join them? In the water."

He takes in the pool lapping about him, shining with light. He lifts his face. "I prefer the water at night . . ."

I follow his gaze. In the opening above, there's a rectangle of night. The galaxy hangs in a vast twinkling aura up there, startlingly clear. I'd prefer that, too.

I can't do anything about it. It rises up, a swish of tender hilarity, getting the better of all my doubts and fears: I laugh. Voper jerks his head at me, and I lift a hand. "I'm sorry. It's just . . . it's funny. That you'd own a yacht and not like the sun. They . . . usually go together."

He stills and says, teeth gritted, "Do I look like somebody who'd enjoy the sun?" Almost, but not quite, a snarl.

I don't know any better, I go on. Look at me now, Mrs. Colding.

For it's hit me. A cool wash of sympathy, spreading through my bones.

The shock of it, to know. To know that a man can have everything, and not be happy.

"You look like you want to be seen," I say at last.

He jerks, that cool, bare face slackening, and turns away, lips instinctively snarling back from white teeth. He makes a sound. What have I done? Then he stands in the pool, wades toward me—I take an involuntary step back—and placing both hands on the edge of the pool, massive muscles cording on his arms, he hauls himself dripping out of the water.

When he straightens he towers over me, huge and lean and deathly pale. I could never tell what kind of body he had under those suits, but it's blindingly clear now. Water channels down between stacked muscles, sheening over puffed-up biceps and a lower abdomen ridged with masculine veins angling toward the groin and into black shorts. Those muscles tell you they were earned. They tell you they can kill.

I take another step back, and Voper leans in toward me, blue eyes hazing black. "I think it's best you go now," he says.

Oh.

How foolish. How very foolish I'd been, after all. To think I could make him change how he thought of me.

I turn and grope away up the stairs, leaving him standing there panting and hands fisted by the pool with its dancing reflections of light.

"Hold up, hold up, hold up," Cailee says as I pace back and forth at the bow, cell to ear. Beyond, the lights of Ajaccio twinkle in the dark. "Why are you so hung up on what he thinks of you?"

"What?" I say, flinging up a hand. "What do you mean? He's the *owner!* Of *course* I have to care about what he thinks of me!"

Cailee sighs. "You do know this is, like, your thing, right?"

I stop pacing. "My *thing?*"

"This is what you did with Josh. You were too worried about what he thought of you to have any confidence in yourself."

I stand there, bottom lip pouting, feeling the beginnings of resentment forming. "That was harsh."

"I'm sorry. But you know it's true. You were always trying to please him."

I put a hand to my brow, suddenly unsteady on my feet as I think of old compromises, backpedaling, accepting slights and gaslighting and fists in order to be in his eyes what I already knew myself to be.

The smothering, tortured patterns of old ways, laid bare before me.

I pinch the bridge of my nose, telling myself Cailee can't know there are tears in my eyes.

But I know she knows, all the same.

Her voice is very gentle when she continues. "Arie. Babe. I just—I feel a little responsible here. I mean, I was the one who dragged you into this, and . . ." I can practically hear her slap her forehead from here. "I wasn't thinking about it, but this is gonna be a *huge* test for you. Like, the whole yachting industry is *about* pleasing people. I can't believe I didn't see it before." She makes an angry noise in her throat. "You're gonna have to be careful. This Voper guy—you don't wanna repeat what you went through with Josh, do you?"

I look down, feeling an unaccountable flush creeping up my neck. "It's not like we're together or anything—"

"I know. Just don't get all wrapped up in what he thinks of you, okay? You're trying to get away from all that. Let it go. Be yourself. Go mate with that hunky first mate."

I snort laughter and nod, wiping at my eyes. "Okay." And I feel a calmness settle in my shoulders, a strength come back into my spine. I lift my chin. "Okay."

NINE

I'm allowed a late start the next day, as I'm on laundry duty. I'm ironing male crew uniforms when Thea comes in with a mound of bed sheets. One look at her face and I know she's got some juicy gossip to share. "What is it?" I say eagerly, and she looks around before leaning in. "It's Lucia."

This'll be good. "What about her?"

"She's gone."

I blink. "What?"

Her eyebrows shoot up: *I know*. "These were from her cabin." She lifts the armful of sheets. "All her stuff was gone. No one's seen her. Poof. I asked around, but Mrs. Colding won't say anything. Word is, Mr. Voper got sick of her and had Jason escort her off the boat during the night."

My jaw drops. "*Wow*."

"Right?" Thea shakes her head. "One thing I know?" She drops the sheets. "Girl was a pig."

She leaves, and I start untangling the white bedding and pause, frowning at a heavy smear of red on them. Is that . . . lipstick?

When I'm relieved for break, I hear the rattling drop of the anchor and go abovedeck to see where the *Lair*'s landed next.

From the looks of it? A pirate cove. The cliffs of Corsica soar up for miles in tumbled crags and pinnacles of red sandstone mantled with maquis scrub. The *Lair* has backed up to them into a little sheltered bay where deep water froths about boulders speckled with the droppings of sea eagles wheeling in the sun-drenched sky. It's absolutely stunning.

I hear the scoffing whine of Emmie on a sun lounger on the swim deck. "But what's stopping us from drifting and smashing up against the cliffs?"

The cool, patient voice of Mrs. Colding replies. "Just wait."

As I watch, the tender idles up to the largest of the boulders in the cove. On the foredeck stands Jason, a thick black stern line in his hands stretching back to the yacht. At the end of the line is a heavy ring of chain-links. He waits for his moment, muscles bunched and skin gleaming gold in the sunlight, and leaps onto the sharp-looking boulder in his bare feet. Emmie and Thea on the swim deck turn to each other, hands hiding their mouths—*hot*—and I shake my head. But my eyes are also drawn to his physique, so well-defined under his tight polo, as he throws the chain like a lasso around the crown of the boulder and snugs it down tight around outcroppings. The sun is beating down on him, and a drop of sweat turns to golden light as it falls from his brow. *How have I never appreciated the male body like this before? For its own sake, separate from the man?* Then Jason has straightened, unclipping his crew radio. "Reel her in, Captain." There's a slow, methodical clanking—the slack anchor-chain getting inched back in—and the stern line begins to rise taut as the *Lair* is towed backwards. The chain suddenly rattles and constricts around the boulder. The stern line hums. And Jason, utterly sure of himself in this world, presses his radio. "Good." The *Lair* is now effectively rendered stationary between two opposing tension points.

I'm snapped out of my reverie by a burst of clapping—Emmie and Thea, standing to applaud. Mrs. Colding seems unimpressed.

I can't help grinning as Jason hops back aboard the *Lair*. "Impressive."

He shrugs, sheepish. "I know how to put on a show for the guests."

I eye him up and down. "That you do."

For a second he stares, and then a laugh leaps out of his throat. "Yeah, well, a hot bod is almost a requirement to get hired as a mate on a boat like this." His ears, I note, have turned very red. "You're pretty much there to be eye candy for the female guests."

"Don't forget the female crew." The rejoinder is out before I can stop myself, or the guilt can set in.

Remember, I think. *You can allow yourself this much.*

Jason, meanwhile, arches a brow. "Oh? Seen any candy about, have you?"

I shrug, nose in the air. "Maybe."

He cracks a grin. "To think I almost let myself be a scrawny bookworm my whole life."

"To think," I tut. "What a waste that would've been."

He regards me for a long moment, the corners of his mouth dimpling in restrained humor. "Miss Strand," he declares at last. "You are starting to emerge."

Cailee's words ringing in my head, I force away all my customary defenses—*Why not have fun?*—and turn to him with lifted chin. "Do you like it?"

He stares at me, all teeth. "Yes. Yes, I do." He rubs his neck, glances about and leans forward. "Hey, I was thinking—"

"Mr. Young." Crew radios whine, and everyone looks up. It is, unmistakably, Mr. Voper's voice. "Meet me in the main salon, please."

I look up, too. Mr. Voper stands under the awning of the aft bridge deck, staring down at us.

Jason unclips his radio. "Right away, sir." He points at me. "Don't go anywhere."

I grin. "Okay."

I look about. Emmie has missed all of this, intent on bossing Thea around. But Mrs. Colding is watching me with a speculative expression.

When Jason returns minutes later he's pale in the face, eyes distant. I approach him with a smile. "So? What were you gonna say?"

He looks at me, opens his mouth—and turns away. "Let's go, boys!" he calls. "Wash that tender down!" And like that, he's gone.

It eases into me like a delayed blow, a creeping, prickling bottoming of my guts. What just happened? And then the queasy humiliation: Was I too forward? Was he not into it?

But Emmie interrupts. Thea is hopping up and down, pointing at a family of dolphins swimming by in sparkling arcs through the water, and Emmie couldn't care less. She groans from her sun lounger, flawless skin glistening with oil, arm flung to brow. "I am so *bored*. We don't even have a yoga instructor onboard."

I unroot myself. *Fuck it*. Here's my chance to get on her good side. "I teach yoga."

She peeks at me from under the shade of her arm. "*Really*."

I square off with her. "Yeah. Internationally certified." I turn to Mrs. Colding. "I could do it now, if I can be spared from my duties for a bit."

Mrs. Colding stares daggers at me.

But Emmie's eyes flick me over. She sits up. "All right, then. Let's do it."

Warm triumph spreads through me.

We do it in the sun on the aft main deck, laying out mats over the closed panels of the pool roof. Everyone changes into leggings and sports bras, as Emmie demands that all the stews participate—out of self-consciousness or wanting an audience, I can't tell which. Mrs. Colding glowers and follows along as if submitting to some humiliation, and a few of the deckhands loiter to watch Emmie stick her ass out in cat cow pose. So an audience, then.

It feels good to teach again; I haven't done it in a while. The instructions flow out calm and clear, and even Emmie listens when I walk about and adjust her posture.

It's only when I'm in cobra pose, arching my back up from the mat with my breasts thrust out, that I lift up my eyes and notice Mr. Voper watching from the shade of the bridge deck overhang.

I instantly blush, faltering in my suddenly too-sexual-feeling pose, and all heads turn to look. The deckhands have suddenly disappeared.

I can't process it at first: Mr. Voper is undoing the buttons of his coat, one by one. He shrugs it off and casually hands it to a passing deckie, begins slipping off his thousand-dollar Italian shoes. "Mind if I join?"

The stews share dumbfounded looks. Apparently, something unprecedented is transpiring.

Mr. Voper raises a brow at my silence.

"Y-Yes," I manage at last. "Be my guest."

He smiles at my phrasing and chooses a mat within the overhang's shade. Waits, barefoot, like some eloping CEO. The sight of him there is so bizarre it takes me a moment to snap out of it. "Um, right." *Let it go, Aurora. Be yourself.* "Plow pose."

He isn't too bad. It's obvious he has never tried yoga in his life, but there is an athletic grace to him that takes to it with startling ease. His presence, however, frays all concentration. Whispers begin and heads constantly turn, as if he were a black hole in the group's center. Emmie doesn't miss the opportunity to play it up, going off-script and trying the puppy dog stretch and wheel pose, arching her ass at him and glancing temptingly over her shoulder. But he ignores her, watching me with an unwavering intensity that is disconcerting. I shift, feeling a flutter between my legs, and when I see Mrs. Colding looking between us with narrowed eyes, it's too much. I stand and begin to circle the class, scrutinizing postures.

After a while, I realize I can't ignore it: Voper's is off.

I cut through the group—heads turn—and come to his side. He's in a kneeling lunge position, back arched and back leg bent, one hand reaching up and behind to grip the foot. He stilts a few fingers to the mat to steady himself. "Here, let's get you back on track," I say, lifting a hand. "I'll show you."

And I touch his shoulder.

There are audible gasps. Mrs. Colding shoots to her feet.

But Voper's eyes only glitter with amusement. Even with him kneeling, I look half his size. I take a breath. "You're strong, but you need to relax your chest." I place a hand there. It's cold, strikingly so, and I think of how I saw him last night, and what's hidden beneath this fitted white business shirt. I swallow and put a hand to his back, gripping his ribcage. The dense, torsional webbing of muscle there is undeniable. "Breathe," I say, and realize I'm saying it more for my sake than for his. I clear my throat. "You're not breathing."

For some reason, this only amuses Voper more. A seam of a smile appears at the corner of his mouth.

I sigh. "A little deeper. Just breathe. Can you breathe for me?"

Voper's face twitches, filling with a sudden, inscrutable nakedness, but he won't look at me. His nostrils flare, his jaw muscles flex. We are very close. I'm barely aware of Emmie watching with mouth hanging in scandalized fury, Mrs. Colding with open fascination. That Captain Redfearn, even, has taken a break from his duties to watch with narrowed eyes and crossed arms.

For I know what's going on here. I know where this kind of tension comes from. Sometimes it feels like I've struggled with it all my life.

I lower my voice. "Mr. Voper." His eyes jerk at me. "Relax. That tension inside? You have to let it go."

He does not look away. Those blue eyes seem to grow larger and larger, searching mine, hauling whatever they need up out of the depths. And I think, *He never blinks.*

Then he sucks in a deep breath, his beastly barrel of a chest expands, and he arches back in a fluid motion, gripping his foot. His form is perfect.

I step away as if released from some sorcery. "Very good."

But when he stands, towering over me, the mask is back in place, his face cold and unapproachable, full of a trembling restraint. Is that . . . disgust?

"Thank you," he says, and curtly nods. "That was . . . edifying."

And he turns and flings open the double doors of the main salon, disappearing inside.

I stand there not knowing what to think, feeling Emmie's eyes burning into the back of my head.

TEN

That night Thea leans against our cabin wall and crosses her arms, a gloating smile on her face. "You two . . ."

I punch my pillow to fluff it, a little too aggressively. "Please just leave me alone."

My thoughts haven't left me alone, though. They very much haven't left me alone. For the rest of the day I'd been all but useless, almost burning every uniform that had come across my ironing board. How could I not turn over, in my mind, every little moment I'd had with Voper that afternoon? How could I not wonder what that expression on his face had meant? What that deep, dangerous tension in his muscles (all those muscles) had meant—

Thea sniggers. "You don't wanna talk about it? I mean, I *definitely* think we should talk about it."

"What's to talk about?" I grouse. "Voper doesn't like me. Hardly breaking news." Thea squints one eye at me, and I glare at her. "What?"

"Nothing," she laughs, shrugging, hands up. "Nothing. Just . . . there seemed to be a connection there."

I shrug now, suddenly self-conscious. "I just . . . could tell. He's carrying a lot of pain."

"Oh?" Thea raises her brows. "You could tell that, could you, from feeling up his hot bod?"

I flush, trying to find the words. "I went through a lot, when I was . . ." I feel a mortifying pressure behind my eyes, and wave a hand. "Anyway, it's why I do yoga. It helps my stress and insomnia. So, I can tell when someone else is also struggling."

"Well," Thea says, thinking that one over. "All I know is, I've never seen Voper do anything like that before." Another ambivalent shrug, and when she climbs up into her bunk I sit there, musing on that.

Sometime in the night I wake with a start, for no reason that's readily apparent. The cabin is dark, the yacht calm and motionless. Just my insomnia, then.

I look up at the cabin doorway to find a familiar shadow there, looking down at me, and the thought thuds through me: *Josh*.

My muscles lock all over. Terror ices my blood. My mind reels.

No. It can't be. He can't have followed—he can't have found me—what is he going to—

But when the shadow steps forward, it's not Josh. It's Voper.

Something flutters and catches behind my breastbone.

Why is he here? What is happening? I shrink back and open my mouth, but his hand is there, his cold pale hand. His blue eyes poison-black in the darkness. My body buzzes, tipped into a tumult of confusion. I should scream, I know. This is wrong. I should fight this. But there is something else in the terror coursing through me. Something depraved and thrilled. He rolls on top of me, and the size of him pressed against me is undeniable. A shivering languidness fills me. My hands open and close, clawing into the sheets. I can't help it, I grind my hips up to meet him, and he lifts away. Bad girl. When he removes his hand from my mouth, he stares at my lips. I stare at his. They're so full, for a man's. Sensuous. I wonder how many women have fallen for those lips.

I suddenly want them.

But one long, pale finger stops my mouth. He dips his head and whispers it into the sensitive shell of my ear: "Relax." His exhalation is cold against my neck. His fingertips glide down me, grazing the sides of my breasts, my ribs, and I quiver. Hidden, neglected parts of me flare to life. I feel a fluttery clench between my legs and realize: I am turned on by Adrian Voper. I *want* Adrian Voper.

I don't care. I pull at him, wanting that delicious weight on me, and I hear a husky, gorgeous grunt of amusement. I can't see his face, his expression, what he thinks of me. All I know is what I can feel pressing against me. He wants me, too. For whatever reason, in this moment, he wants me.

I won't waste it. I grab at him, whispering it, begging it, "Please." I hear him groan, and the thought of me causing him to lose control makes me tingle. I grab a fistful of his hair and pull him to my breasts. I know what he wants. I know what will make him happy. His hands float down me and buttons pop, fabric falls away. He's peeling me like some rare delicacy. I'm being devoured. I've never, ever been wanted like this, and I'm so turned on I want to scream. How can Thea not hear us? How can she not know what's happening to my world?

And then—no—he's gone, the weight has left me, but only so he can roll me onto my side. I feel him pressed against my ass, his hands filled with my breasts, and I shut my eyes. *Dear God.* I grind back against it, wanting it. He chuckles deep in his throat and it's tipping me over the edge. Then his voice is in my ear again. "Relax," he growls. "You have to let it go." I feel a wetness spreading, a wetness that is not me, and open my eyes. The bunk is soaked, water is spreading over the sheets all around us, dripping onto the floor. And when I look over my shoulder at Voper, he's shirtless, white as a corpse, in the same swimming trunks he wore in the pool. He smiles. "Breathe," he says, his mouth sharp, and bites my neck . . .

I wake rigid in bed and jerk my hand away from my damp underwear. I'm so turned on I'm practically writhing, so unnerved I have to clamp a hand over my mouth. Where is he?

No. No. Just a dream.

Jesus.

What the fuck was that?

I suck in a breath, cheekbones burning red in the dark, and try to decide how much of my emotions are shame, how much arousal. If I only dreamt him wanting me, or if he really does in this strange, waking world.

ELEVEN

My thoughts are heavy and slow, my hands shaky as I go about my morning makeup routine. I start with a light moisturizer, then a waterproof foundation (perfect for yachties) that I apply with my fingertips and blend out with a damp sponge. I set everything with a translucent powder, a bronzer in a butterfly shape around my face, and go about applying my finishing touches of mascara, blusher, lipstick. I study myself in the mirror as I do, eyes gliding over dark hair, freckle-dusted nose, the questionable plumpness of my lips. Judging. Assessing. And then I realize: I've spent double the time I usually do on my makeup this morning. This is a ritual. A preparation.

I've been thinking of last night's dream the whole time.

I drop my hands, jaw clenching. What am I doing? Maybe Cailee was right. Maybe I'm falling back into old habits. It's not even been a month, and already I'm fantasizing about another guy who's abusive. How fucked up am I?

Sure, I haven't been touched by a man in a while. Not since Josh. But a wet dream, about Voper of all people?

I dump my makeup back into my bag and head up to the crew mess.

At the top of the stairs I'm confronted by a spiral of hair that bewitches the eye, a perfect French twist that has a vertiginous power to it. I know this hair, this severe coiffure, but it's all wrong. It's not blonde. It's a witchy black.

The coiffure revolves, and Mrs. Colding turns around to take me in.

"Ah, there you are, Miss Strand." Her icy gaze sweeps me head to foot in curious evaluation. Behind her, four angrily gossiping clones of myself turn to glare at me and the fact whams home: All the stews have dyed their hair the exact same shade as mine.

I shift my weight uncertainly. "What—what's going on—"

"Let's not dawdle," Mrs. Colding submits sharply, and turns her gleaming stranger's head. "Girls. I'm sure we all have duties to attend to."

A silence, a shuffling of feet, and the stews file out, giving me poisonous looks. Even Thea eyes me warily.

When they're gone, I say it. "Mrs. Colding?" My voice wavers. "Please tell me what's going on."

Mrs. Colding steps close and looks down her long nose at me, cups my chin in her hand. I stand perfectly still. I haven't seen this expression from her before. Wonder, perhaps, or pity. The beginnings, too, of respect. It's absolutely terrifying. "Come," she says, and her voice is the softest it has ever been. "Let's see how you do serving today."

The guests have requested breakfast on the bridge deck, outdoors in the shade of the overhang. I follow Mrs. Colding and Thea from the galley, down service stairs and out onto the deck, a wooden charger in my hands. My fingers are slick with sweat, my heart fluttering. Last night's dream must be written all over my face as I approach the long dining table. Voper sits at its end, Emmie beside him. He is wearing his usual dark suit, but today no tie throttles his neck, and the top few buttons of his white business shirt are undone. The change is strangely startling.

When his eyes flick up at me, I nearly drop my charger.

He takes a thick cut of steak this morning, red and rare, swimming in blood and juices. He attacks it nicely, easily, his knife gliding through the meat as if it were melting, never hacking or sawing as most men do, and I wonder how I ever thought those long, pale hands were womanly. I think of them on me, gripping me, weighing me, and look up to find his eyes on me again.

Does he know what I'm thinking, what's happened to me? Does he know I want his mouth on me, tasting me, biting me?

Emmie has been coldly watching me this whole time. Her eyes dart between my hair and the other stews', Mr. Voper's eyes and mine. She lifts an oyster out of a bucket of ice and lemon wedges on the half-shell and swallows it down whole, tosses the shell aside. "I see the country girl is serving us today," she comments idly, flicking her fingers.

Voper's knife does not pause. I feel a sick twisting in my guts and Mrs. Colding glances at me, purses her lips. "She is coming along nicely."

"Is that so?" Another oyster goes back, and Emmie washes it down with a swallow of champagne.

"Is there something you wanted to say, dear?" Voper poses in a soft voice, eyes still on his plate.

Emmie shrugs, a grotesquely exaggerated gesture. "Oh, nothing. I was just surprised you'd let someone like her onboard. What with her foot fetish and all."

I shut my eyes, ears burning. I will myself to sink into the teak deck. Disappear. Mrs. Colding flashes me a withering look, but Voper only dabs at his lips with a handkerchief. "Foot fetish? Do tell."

Emmie luxuriates in my agony, eyes gloating. "Oh, didn't I tell you? Apparently, this little farm girl here has been dying to know what the rich life is like. My first day onboard I found her trying on my pumps. My *Stuart Weitzman* pumps."

Mrs. Colding's face is like a glacier imploding. Thea's eyes are lowered. Voper's, however, lift to my face now. His expression is inscrutable. "Is that right?"

Desperate, unprepared excuses bubble out of me. "Mr. Voper, I was just—"

"Being creepy? Snooping around?" Another half-shell clacks onto the table, and Emmie wipes her fingers on her gossamer pareo. "She always did obsess over me in high school. I guess she never outgrew it." She dangles her champagne glass in one hand with bimboish elegance, leans back in her chair. "Only question is"—her gimlet eyes narrow at me—"do we really need someone that unprofessional onboard?"

Trembling silence. I can hardly breathe. I have one hand to my stomach, holding in the nerves. Thea looks like she's about to bolt.

At last, Mrs. Colding rouses. "Mr. Voper, I take full responsibility—"

But Mr. Voper lifts a pale, tapered hand. His eyes, resting on me, glitter with amusement. "I think we can indulge a little curiosity, don't you?"

Emmie's jaw drops. Even through the dizzying lightheadedness that follows, I want to frame her expression. It. Is. *Priceless.*

"*What?*" She splutters. "She—she tried on *my shoes.* I've seen you fire a chef for not placing the *garnish* properly—"

Mr. Voper turns a mild eye on her. "Are you questioning my judgment?"

And that perfect jaw sucks up with a click. Goodbye.

I don't know whether I want to cry, or faint, or burst out in laughter as Mr. Voper goes back to eating his steak.

I'm on eggshells for hours afterwards. I help clear breakfast, send linens to the laundry. The other stews take care to avoid me, whispering to each other as they pass. I'm a genuine sensation now, the only worthy topic of conversation: Aurora Strand, maritime melodrama.

Even Thea, it seems, has turned against me.

"Hey," I say when I pass her with an armload of laundry. "I don't know what you think, but I didn't—"

"Uh-huh," she mutters. And then, over her shoulder, "Whatever a girl needs to do to get ahead, right?"

My eyes sting with tears.

I'm doing dishes in the galley when Mrs. Colding walks in. I stiffen, waiting for the withering comment to come, but she merely presses her lips together. "Miss Gallagher requests to see you in her cabin," she states and stalks away.

What? That's it? Mrs. Colding doesn't believe in a good old-fashioned keel-hauling?

But she stops, turns back. "I trust I need not point out how very thin the ice is you're standing on, Miss Strand. If you screw up again and cannot make the guests happy . . ." And she leaves the sentence dangling, devastatingly, in the air.

Yeah. That's more like it.

I knock and enter to find Emmie waiting on the edge of her huge fuckdoll bed, long legs crossed. She's changed into a flowy cream pantsuit and oversized waist sash. A clear power move.

High-stakes high fashion on the high seas, here we go.

"Emmie," I begin. "I'm sorry if—"

But Emmie holds a finger to her lips—"Shh"—and smiles a frozen smile behind it.

I gulp.

She rises up like a lanky statue of femininity and paces around me, carefully analyzing my face and body. My ass, my breasts (different sizes, natch), my height (five feet four inches, baby!), my dark hair. She shakes her head. "What does he see in you?"

My head juts forward like a vulture in confusion. "Who?"

Emmie scoffs, studying me with undisguised malice. "Do you think I don't know what you're doing? Did you really think I'd let you *win?* Voper is *mine.* I have worked my *ass* off to get where I am. I have preened, and stripped, and debased myself to the masses to get on this boat with this man, and I won't let some farmyard slut like you swoop in at the last minute and take him from me. He is *my* ticket to a better life. *Mine.*"

"How romantic," I quip under my breath.

Emmie's face colors. "*What* did you say?"

Shit. I've really gone and done it now, haven't I? Why can't I keep my stupid mouth shut?

But I can't go back. The blood roars in my ears as I look her straight in the eyes. "He deserves better than you."

We're inches apart now. I can feel her panting breath on my face. Her pupils narrow, lips curling back from gritted teeth. And just like that, she composes herself. That glimpse of beastly womanhood? Gone. She saunters over to a plate, returns with something cradled in her palm. She brims with sympathy, commiseration, motherly concern. "You must be *so* hungry, working so hard for us silly guests with our tempers. Here." She offers whatever it is to me like an eager flower child, enunciating the two words with chilling courtesy: "Eat this."

A stinky, fishy funk wafts up at me. It's an oyster, its meat cloudy and shriveled in the half-shell. I swallow. "Is that . . . from breakfast?"

"Just eat it." I look at her and her expression changes, voice dangerously low. "You think the shoe thing got you in hot water? What do you think they'd do if they found out you were refusing a guest?"

But I shake my head, a wave of disgust washing over me, drowning out my fear. "I'm not eating that."

A pulse tics in one of Emmie's eyelids, giving her a slightly deranged look. A delicate spite creeps into her voice. "And what if I told them you were stealing my stuff?"

My jaw hangs in a silent, appalled gasp. "You wouldn't . . ."

She grins all her perfect teeth, shining with vicious glee. "Oh, but I would."

It's suddenly hard to breathe. I bite my lip, thinking of Mrs. Colding, of the end of Mr. Voper's patience.

Of never seeing Voper again.

I take the oyster.

Cold triumph snags Emmie's lips as I weigh it in my hand. My stomach heaves at the rank smell, but I force it down. I tip my head and slurp the cold mollusk back, tentatively chew. It's beyond awful. I gag, and Emmie points a finger. "Don't you *dare* vomit on this carpet. *Eat it.*" I brace my hands on my knees, grinding through gritty, salty brininess. It exudes foulness into my head like alcohol vapor. "That's right. All of it," Emmie seethes into my ear. "Swallow that shit." I gulp it down, gasping, and she smiles. "See? That wasn't so bad, was it?"

I look up at her, eyes tearing. I didn't know. That evil could be so petty. Nothing grand about it at all.

Just a jealous little model in a pantsuit.

"Miss Strand?" The familiar, slightly surprised voice emanates behind us, and Emmie straightens, blazing an innocent smile over my shoulder. When I turn around, Voper is watching me with something that could almost be mistaken for concern, and I realize for the first time: He really is the most beautiful man I have ever seen.

He lifts a brow. "Is everything all right?"

Emmie's fingers dig into my arm, and I dutifully smile. "Yeah. Just . . . girls bonding, you know."

Voper glances between us, brow furrowed. *Uh-huh.* Then steps forward and holds out a sleek black credit card.

I stare.

"Oh, did I forget to tell you?" Emmie simpers innocently, touching my shoulder. "I asked for some clothes, and I thought you could be a dear and pick them up for me."

There's also a note. It's an address: *Hermès, La Piazza, 07021 Porto Cervo, Sardinia, Italy.*

Emmie is glowing with barely restrained glee when I look up at Voper. "But—this is in Sardinia—"

"The helicopter will take you there," Adrian explains. "It should only be"—he glances at a ridiculously expensive-looking watch—"about five hours round-trip."

Emmie drapes herself on him like a cashmere sweater. "We'll be here when you get back. Try not to dirty my clothes with your peasant fingers, will you?" And she smirks in smug triumph as she shuts the door in my face.

TWELVE

My first helicopter ride begins with me holding back tears.

The ferocious thwop, thwop, thwop of the rotor blades jolts me down to my toes, chattering my teeth. The pilot glances over at me, at the glassiness threatening to spill down my cheeks, but I fix my eyes on the azure incandescence of the Mediterranean spread before us and after a while he turns back to his controls. I wonder if I scream whether it will be lost in the deafening noise or not. And then I want to laugh. At one time this experience, this undreamt-of luxury, would have been thrilling. But that is gone. Now? It's like being flown to my own execution. To a place I've known I would always go. That voice wakens in me, that voice that is always there, that in depressive episodes is like a siren's call, dragging me disbelieving onto the rocks. *You do not matter*, it says. *You never mattered. You thought there was something there? There is nothing there. Women like her will always get what they want. Women like you? Well. This is what happens to them. Packed off, sent off, sent on errands, like a dog. This is what they deserve. This is what you deserve. You were never good enough.*

My old, damaged self, unpacked and waiting for me, asking wherever did I go.

Porto Cervo is like a birthday cake: all white and candy-pink stucco buildings with terracotta roofs, a delirious playground for the rich summoned up on the Sardinian coast. I march into Hermès in a daze. The few patrons—a gaggle of women who look like fixtures on the Chanel runway—stop and stare at me in my polo and deck shoes as if I were a dog turd on the sidewalk. Great. More models. Just what I wanted.

But it doesn't stop there. The saleswoman behind the front case is also a vertically affluent fashionista, and makes no effort to disguise her own disgust. She actually wrinkles her nose as she looks me over.

"Can I help you?"

"Yeah," I say, and lift my chin. "I'm here to pick up a purchase for Adrian Voper."

The saleswoman blinks. "Oh."

Minutes later, another clerk glides out from the back holding no less than eight shopping bags. I gape as they're hung on my arms. Seriously? And then the receipt: over $40,000.

My face is a mask of dead-eyed fury as I'm choppered back to the yacht. The pilot knows better than to try to get my attention now.

The long, humiliating walk to Emmie's VIP suite. My arms are burning by the time I stand before the door. I take a breath, lift a hand and knock. Emmie's excited footsteps are loud and immediate. The door swings in and those puffy, plumped lips part in delighted scorn as she takes in the extravagant shopping spree dangling from my arms. She arches a shoulder girlishly. "Baby, you shouldn't have!" she squeals, and painted nails reach out—

"I didn't," says a lazy voice behind her. Voper appears—my eyes instantly check for signs of his clothes being rumpled, and find none—and he puts his hands in his pockets. "Did I say those were for you?"

Emmie freezes, her breath coming out as an uncomfortable, tittering laugh. "What do you mean?"

He inclines his head and explains it as if to a child. "Those are for Aurora."

I blink, the words echoing nonsensically in my ears: *Those are for Aurora.* What did that mean? That surely did not mean—

But Emmie grasps it before I do. The horror on her face is exquisite. "You must be joking."

And Voper looks straight at me. "A country girl deserves a little sophistication here and there, doesn't she?" I can only stare back, feeling as if all the air has been sucked out of me. Is it true, then? Could he possibly—do those crinkled eyes actually mean he—

And he dips a hand into one of the bags stuffed with crinkly wrapping tissue and lifts out a familiar, diamond-encrusted Stuart Weitzman pump. "I trust this will satisfy any more curious urges?" he says. Is this a rebuke? Before I can answer he drops the pump back into the bag and slips past, hands in pockets, a grin or scowl on his face, I can't tell which. "I'll be in the sauna."

His footsteps fade, and Emmie and I are left staring at each other. Thrumming silence. Then her face contorts into a harpy's and she slams the cabin door. An enraged scream comes from behind it. Then a crashing, the sound of furniture being overturned, porcelain shattering against a wall. I blink, turn and find Mrs. Colding standing rigid in the passageway. She eyes me up and down, the Hermès bags on my arms. The door. "What is . . ." she begins, and I shake my head. "I don't know. I don't know what's happening right now."

She draws herself up, suddenly peremptory. "Stow those in the other VIP suite, and then go down to the sauna to see if Mr. Voper needs anything."

"Yes, ma'am," I mumble and scurry away. I don't need to be told twice.

When I look back Mrs. Colding is standing in front of the cabin door, hands calmly clasped before her, as if waiting on a friend drunk in the restroom at the club.

Much sooner than I'm ready for, I'm walking down the passageway on the lower deck to the sauna. My hands twist at themselves. I feel hot and flushed. I know I should be worried about Emmie; there's no way she's not going to make the rest of this trip a living nightmare for me. But nevertheless, it persists: an undercurrent of excitement, of exquisite delight, impossible to ignore.

He bought the clothes for me.

And more than that, almost too much to bear—he said it. He said my first name, savoring it in that perfect mouth of his as if it were a delicacy.

Those are for Aurora.

My hands are shaking when I peek through the glass door of the sauna.

But no one's inside, just billowings of steam and sweating cedar boards. Empty.

He must be in the snow room, then. I open the outer glass door, but pause before the heavy inner one. Do I really need to check on him while he's in there? It somehow seems more private. But Mrs. Colding said . . .

I sigh, shaking my head, and pull the huge wooden door wide.

A blast of icy cold hits me, setting my teeth chattering, and I blink through vapors at the beards of snow hanging from the slabs of black stone inside. No one there. "Hello?" I hazard. "Mr. Voper?" I creep forward, peering around the corner in the L-shaped winter cavern, and there he is. He sits on a stone perch with his back to the wall, eyes shut, hands in lap. He is completely naked. I stiffen, breath held. Snow dusts his brambled black hair, his broad, bulky shoulders, his arms, his knees, but does not melt. No shivering from him, he does not even have a towel. He seems as if he has been there forever, a strange arctic effigy. A *naked* effigy. How does he not have hypothermia?

His vivid blue eyes open, blinking snow off those beautiful lashes as they look up at me. "You're snooping again, Aurora."

I would blush if my blood was still moving. I jerk my eyes away. "I—sorry. Mrs. Colding said to check on you . . ."

"I am fine. Thank you." His lips curve.

"Okay." I hover, not sure where to put my eyes, flooded with embarrassment as I hug my arms. "I, uh, wanted to thank you. No one's ever . . ."

He lets me flounder, as if enjoying the spectacle. And then, finally sparing me, "You're welcome."

How is his formality so sexy?

"Okay," I say again. "I'll . . . be outside."

And I retreat, hurrying past the sauna, the spa, into the passageway toward the beach club. Away.

Wow, Arie. Can you get any more awkward?

And still my thoughts linger on his body. On the fine line of hair beneath his bellybutton, descending down to . . .

Stop it, Aurora.

I flutter my hands, trying to get warmth back into them. My head feels hot. Hotter than it should, anyway. I'm still trying to figure that out when I hear spiky, bitchy footsteps approaching. Even Mrs. Colding doesn't have such vitriol in her step.

Here we go. Supermodel vs. stewardess.

Emmie's in a flowy silk shirt that's unbuttoned to show she's got nothing on underneath but a sexy black bikini bottom, all the good parts hanging out. Of course.

Emmie Gallagher: in it to win it.

"Congratulations, farm girl," she singsongs, "you're Voper's charity case of the week." She lets the shirt slide off her perfectly perky tits and holds it up for me to take. Her moist, harlot-red lips purse in a kiss of scorn. "But I am going to give that man the best blowjob he's ever had," she announces with airy conviction, "and afterwards he's going to come out and tell you you're done on this boat." She leans a hand on the tall mirrors lining the passageway and takes it away, holding it to her mouth. *Oopsy.* "I'm sorry, do you have to wipe that down now?" And she walks on, trailing a hand along the mirrors all the way, leaving a smeary handprint down twenty feet of glass in a screeching dragging of skin. She looks back with a coquettish smile.

My shoulders heave. I am boiling over with useless rage, my head ready to explode. Or is that a headache? I put a hand to my brow and it comes away shining with sweat. What's going on? Everything feels weird. Then a wave of nausea hits me, doubling me over, hands on knees and shivering like a sick horse, and Emmie pauses in her march of triumph. "Oh, goody," she calls back. "The food poisoning is kicking in." And she swings wide the glass door of the snow room, perfect brow arched. "Have fun with that."

THIRTEEN

My jaw drops in utter disbelief as I think back on that awful oyster. That conniving little . . .

But another wave of nausea nearly knocks me over, and I start hustling up to the main deck. I need to get to my cabin. Into bed. I need . . .

"And what exactly are you doing here?" Mrs. Colding stands in the middle of the main lounge, iPad in hand. Her voice is the hiss of a viper. "Did you leave Mr. Voper alone?"

My stomach plummets. "I'm sorry, Mrs. Colding. I—I'm not feeling well—"

"This may be a surprise to you, Miss Strand, but I have no interest in your emotional dilemmas—"

"No, really. Emmie, she—"

A loud sigh. "I am quite done with the theatrics between the two of you. If you cannot be professional—"

"But Mrs. Colding—"

"*Miss Strand.*" Mrs. Colding's eyes blaze. "If you do not return to your post immediately, this boat will leave port without you. Is that clear?"

I swallow, head pounding. "Yes, ma'am," I manage meekly, and head back to the spa area like a whipped dog.

Okay, then. Yes. That should not have been surprising. This is what it means to be a stewardess, after all.

Chin up, Aurora. Be professional.

In no time at all I'm back in that hateful, gleaming spa again. I polish away Emmie's smeary handprint on the wall mirrors, taking my time, knowing any vigorous exertion will end in me projectile vomiting all over that beautiful glass. When I'm done I step back, taking in my work. The person reflected back at me is swaying, sheened in sweat, tendrils of flyaway hair sticking to her temples.

I'll be fine. Whoever that is will be fine.

S'all good.

After a while it comes to me: It's been a long time, and they haven't come out of the snow room yet. No one stays in a snow room that long. Three minutes, tops? Hasn't it been ten already?

I should check on them.

I shuffle to the door. The distance is only a few yards, but it telescopes claustrophobically before me. How am I to get there without hurling all over my shoes? But, magically, I do. I swing the outer glass door wide and it bumps me in the ass as I stagger through. I plunk my forehead on the huge wooden inner door. "Mr. Voper?" I call. I'm the most unenthusiastic babysitter ever. "Do you need anything?"

Please. Just shout at me. Tell me I'm interrupting the best blowjob you've ever had.

But he doesn't. Only silence greets me. Groaning, I haul open the door.

I fully expect to see Emmie crouching before him, for the worst image ever to be scorched onto my retinas. But I don't.

Instead I see a pair of bare legs poking around the corner in that L-shaped winter wonderland.

My brow furrows. "Emmie?" I call, softly, searing cold diving into my lungs. I shuffle forward, my breath fogging in the air. I must know something is wrong by now, because I don't call again.

My legs do not buckle when I see it. It is laid out all very clearly before me, as if it were a tableau to be admired. Emmie's splayed body, her wide, surprised but drunken-looking eyes. Her throat torn open as if by some beast. The blood, the great red shock of it, gleaming down her breasts and in the obscene whiteness of all that snow.

Emmie, don't worry. You'll be famous now.

You've been taken care of.

I make it outside the snow room before I'm on my knees and am violently sick. I'm crying, I'm sobbing up dribbles of puke. I wipe my mouth and fumble for my crew radio. "Mrs. Colding," I rasp. "Mrs. Colding. Get down here, please." And there she is, like a mirage. How is all this happening so fast? Her face is very white as I point. And I tell her. I tell her the fact that is splitting my world in two. Emmie. In there. Dead.

Why don't you go see?

Mrs. Colding's brows pinch together. She looks at the puddle of vomit before me and seems to come to some conclusion, kneels and touches my shoulder. And that's when she tells me something that sends the blood shocking into my ears.

Emmie left the boat.

I stare. I blink. It is impossible. "*What?*" I hoarse. My voice is jarring, loud and bright to my ears.

Mrs. Colding nods. "Jason got her a cab in port just a few minutes ago. She . . . had an argument with Mr. Voper. She's gone."

Alive.

I look about. The other stews have gathered in the passageway behind, Thea foremost among them, all with naked worry stamped on their faces. The wild edge to my squawk in the radio must have brought them all running.

I shake my head. "No. That . . . that can't be . . ." I push to my feet and brush past Mrs. Colding's outstretched arms to the snow room. And she's right: There's no body there. No blood staining the snow. No murder.

What did I see?

I back away, whirling. Everywhere, concerned faces. Everywhere, disbelief. *Are you okay, Aurora? Everything all right?*

No. No, everything is not all right. How can it be, when I am questioning my reality?

"But, I *saw* it," I splutter. "She was *right there* . . ."

And then Mrs. Colding is there, gripping my shoulders. Her words shear through the black silence that is vibrating around me. "You said you were feeling unwell?"

I swallow, feeling cornered. "Food . . . food poisoning . . ." I mutter, and the words bring on another wave of nausea.

"Well that's just it, then, isn't it?" Mrs. Colding encourages. There's a jauntiness to her tone now, of almost relief. A problem has been solved, a sane solution presented.

I'm feverish. Merely saw something that wasn't there. Yes?

No. How could such a thing—the enormity of such a thing—happen only in my head? How was it not real?

Emmie Gallagher, dead. Emmie Gallagher, with her throat torn open.

Perhaps this is how it happens. This is the moment they talk about. The deep, dark slide into a place you can never get out of.

This is how you go insane.

"No. No," I say as the stewardesses back warily away, eyeing me like an escaped animal. The humiliation is welling up, followed by a stubborn, childish defiance. I shake my hands, eyes blurring. "She was *there*. And Voper . . ."

And there he is, striding toward me. Impeccably dressed, brow furrowed in concern. I back away. "No . . ." And then the world is spinning, I'm falling and there are strong arms holding me, lifting me up. Another hallucination, then. For Voper wouldn't care about little ole me. He would never do that. He would never carry me through that staring crowd, as he is now, barking at everyone to get out of his way. He would never look down at me as if I am the most important thing in his world. He would never . . .

FOURTEEN

I watch the clean, strong line of Voper's jaw as the world floats by. I am suspended, lulled into a disbelieving surrender. I am in a dream. My eyelids are heavy; blackness comes for me, recedes, comes again. Voper speaks, he is speaking to Mrs. Colding. "Get a doctor," he growls. "Now. I don't care how, fly one in." The anger pulses out of him, I can feel it in his chest like the fire beneath a mountain. I lay my cheek against it and try to think. To think of what has happened. Things are going back to being themselves again, outrageous fancies reverting to facts in my head. I see Emmie Gallagher, the blood ungeysering back into her throat, stalking out of the snow room and on to the dock, hailing a cab. Alive.

Thanks for the food poisoning, Emmie.

And still, a fantasy remains: I am being carried by Adrian Voper through the interior of a yacht in the Mediterranean. How can that be real?

"You're real," I say, poking Voper's chest, and stub my finger on the unyielding solidity of his pectoral. "Ow."

He looks down at me, confused. "Yes."

"So where're we going? You gonna dump me overboard so you can finally be rid of me?"

His brow creases. "What?"

I leave my hand on his chest. I'm stroking him. "Why are you in these suits all the time, anyway? They're like a uniform."

He seems to think this over, genuinely stumped. "I've never thought about it."

"You look better out of them, anyway," I comment, and put a hand over my eyes. Apparently, I vomited out my filter along with the oyster. "Did I just say that?"

He nods, mouth quirking. "Afraid so."

I look around. We're on the main deck now, going through the lounge. Avid eyes are watching us. A passing deckie stops and gapes.

I hide my face against Adrian's chest. "Oh my God, get me out of here."

He considers me a moment, eyebrows pinching together. "Okay." He glides to a wall and nudges a cornice with his elbow. Before I know it, a panel has slid back and we're in a dark, narrow corridor. A secret passageway. I blink. "Seriously? Don't tell me you use this to spy on your lady friends . . ."

He grimaces, jaw tight. "No."

Another bump of the elbow, and another panel pops out. We're in one of the VIP suites. "I knew it!" I exclaim, fist pumping, and my stomach heaves. I clutch it. "Bathroom," I squeak, and he lets me down so I can dash to the toilet just in time to void an endless stream of vomit. "Oh God," I groan, waving. "Don't come in here."

But his hand is on my back, rubbing in tiny, hesitant circles.

I flush, vomit, flush again, splash water on my face in the sink and regard myself in the mirror. I'm a ghastly, bluish gray, fevered eyes insane with smudged mascara. Behind me Voper, infuriatingly, looks perfect. "You look awful, Aurora," he says, face tight.

"Gee, thanks." I cup a hand under the faucet and ladle water on my neck, regard my reflection once more. "I'm like the undead," I huff, and Voper's face pinches.

"Come on," he says. "Let's get you to bed."

But I shake my head—*Uh-uh*—and dive to the toilet again. I'm halfway crying by the time I'm done. I curl up on the floor around the toilet. This is where I belong. I'm going to stay here forever. God, I must be the most unattractive thing on two legs he's ever seen. "I don't think I can go anywhere," I groan.

"Aurora—"

"Please," I whine. "Just leave me here. Just leave me here . . ." And darkness comes.

When I come to, he's carrying me again. Jesus, I like being carried by him. I could get used to this. Then my stomach lurches. "I'm not feeling so great," I pontificate, as if this is just occurring to me, and Voper snorts. He lays me on the bed and I sink into it. It's the softest thing I've ever felt. I love you, bed.

Voper pulls the covers over me and I push at him. "Why are you being so nice to me?"

"Hush. Drink this." He's holding a water bottle to my lips. I shake my head, but he ignores me and I gulp it down. Fine.

Exhaustion settles on me like a warm blanket. My eyelids droop as I regard him leaning over me. "You're not here," I state sleepily.

"Okay, you win. I'm not here," he replies. There's a smile in his voice.

I take that smile with me into my dreams.

I'm vomiting. Adrian Voper is holding a champagne bucket under my face, my loosened hair gathered back in his fist. I squeeze my eyes shut. "This is so embarrassing," I manage between convulsions. "How are you not—"

"Hush," he replies and I drift off, shuddering and slick with sweat, while he presses something cold and damp to my face.

When I wake, I jerk to see a figure leaning over me in the dimness. "Shh," Voper says. "It's me." His suit jacket is gone, his shirtsleeves rolled up to the elbows. All in all, he looks disturbingly comfortable perched on the edge of my bed.

Before I can form some kind of protest, he lifts my head and places two pills on my tongue, waits for me to swallow water before lowering me back. Then he places a hand on my forehead. It's blissfully cool. "Here. Let's check that temperature."

"I'm such an idiot," I try to say, but it comes out garbled around the thermometer he's put in my mouth. "I can't believe I let Emmie force me into eating that oyster."

Voper's face is grim, the muscles dancing in his jaw. "If you're not careful, you're going to eat the thermometer too," he admonishes quietly.

When he takes it out and checks it, I ask, "This is over, isn't it?" My chest is hard and tight. "You're going to fire me. I can't work. I'm useless to you now—"

His eyes flash. "Don't be silly."

The brusqueness, the almost considerate dismissive tone, silences me for a moment. But only a moment. It's not enough. I need more.

"Why don't you have one of the stews doing this? Why are you—"

"The doctor should be here soon," he says, almost a growl, and fusses with the covers. "You should get some rest." He sweeps a thumb across my brow, gently, and I wonder how that's supposed to check my temperature. His eyes don't belong to the Voper I know.

"You never get tucked in, do you?" I say at last. I sound like a child.

He scowls. Not a favorite subject. "I don't think you want to know about my sleeping habits," he warns.

"So we're both insomniacs? That sounds promising."

"Does it?" He is amused.

I nod, lift a finger and touch his nose. "It does."

He looks at me, eyes jerking in surprise. As if no one, as long as he has been Adrian Voper, billionaire entrepreneur, has ever done this. And probably no one has. The corner of his mouth curls. A vein throbs on his brow. There's a swelling girth to his neck, as if he is holding something in. When it comes, I am not ready for it. It beats into my face like a wind. Into my face, my head, pulling everything to rags.

Adrian Voper's laughter.

It is as if light is piercing out of him. That smooth, pale face breaks into smile lines I want to dive into and live in forever. He is glowing. That tortured, tragic air about him has vanished, blown away by the breath coming out of him in huge, husky gusts of air. He cannot hold it in, the cabin echoes with it. I am dazzled by his smile. By the person that has been hiding behind that cold mask all this time.

How have I never heard this before? How can I live now without hearing it?

And I know. I know I have never seen anything so beautiful as Adrian Voper's happiness. I know I have become instantly and irrevocably addicted to it.

This I also know: that I have passed through a gate and it has clanged shut behind me, cutting off all that has come before. And here I am, gliding on, smooth and intact, and sparkling with possibility.

When he is done, when that lovely rumbling has passed, Adrian Voper wipes at his eyes and says, "Well. That hasn't happened in a long time."

And he looks at me and places one cool, pale hand to my cheek like a benediction.

FIFTEEN

I wake to voices. My head is pounding and groggy, I don't know what time it is. The curtains are drawn, the cabin dark as the pit. The door is open a crack and in the slice of light I catch a glimpse of two figures in the passageway outside. The voices are hushed, and I know immediately this is a conversation I am not meant to hear.

"I won't do it," says a voice with chilly froideur—Mrs. Colding.

"Please." Unmistakably Voper. There's a pleading tone there I have not heard before.

But Mrs. Colding won't have it. "I know what this is, and I'll have no part of it."

What is *it*?

"I don't—" A sigh. I'm sure he's just put his hands in his pockets. "I'm afraid of what will happen to her."

I am shivering now.

"Is that the only thing you're afraid of?" Mrs. Colding sniffs. "You're not afraid of feeling again?" A long pause follows. When she speaks again, the cool sympathy in her voice denotes a role that extends well beyond chief stewardess. "I won't. I won't see her disposed of like the others. She's different, and you know it."

Me. She is talking about me.

She is *defending* me.

Her. Mrs. Colding.

Voper makes a noise of protest, but she interrupts. "I've seen what you're like around her, Adrian. Don't think I haven't. I've seen what's she done to you. She's the best thing that's happened to you in a long time."

I lie very still. There's a beating in my ears, a cavity in my chest. I don't know what to think. I have been waylaid. I have been wrapped up in radiant consolation.

"I am done with this conversation," Mrs. Colding is saying. "You will give her a chance, and that's that. I'll see you tomorrow, Mr. Voper." Swift, punishing footsteps. She's gone.

My heart is hammering now. After a long moment the slice of light widens and I shut my eyes. He is watching me from the door.

He is so quiet he must have flowed across the room like liquid, because I do not hear him until he lowers himself into the chair beside the bed. My thoughts are hurtling about, I don't know if I can ever sleep again. But I do. I sleep, and dream. I dream of Adrian Voper sitting at my bedside, watching over me.

I wake to a polite rap on the door. I jerk up, holding the covers to my chest, and look over at the chair beside the bed—but it's empty. I swallow back disappointment. "Come in."

Mrs. Colding breezes into the dim cabin with a breakfast tray. "Good morning," she says with tempered aloofness. "How are you feeling?"

"Better. I think." I hold a hand to my brow, and remember Voper's hand there.

Mrs. Colding sets the breakfast tray before me. "The doctor said you'd be fine in a day or so. Just need to keep liquids in you."

"I don't even remember him coming by."

Mrs. Colding wipes her hands on her skirt. "I suppose you wouldn't, you were quite out of it. Mr. Voper was worried." She goes to the curtains and I squint as they're drawn back in a glare of sunshine. The sea stretches beyond the massive windows, chipped into diamonds of glittering light.

That's when I see the note on the breakfast tray.

My heart thuds as I pick it up. The handwriting is in tall, elegant cursive: *Rest up. Take your time. Perhaps we'll bump into each other later, wandering the boat at some strange hour.*

So it's a date, then.

My hands are trembling when I set the note back down.

Mrs. Colding has turned from the curtains and is watching me with an expression I can't pin down. "I'll check on you in a few hours," she declares. "Rest. Take a shower. Change your clothes." She gestures at the cabin's walk-in wardrobe, and I see the horde of Hermès shopping bags I left there yesterday.

I look at her. "I don't understand. How long am I to rest for?"

She merely stares at me, so I try again.

"What about my job? When am I—"

"You don't need to worry about that." She is brisk and businesslike, as if we are discussing a purely trivial matter. As if my life has not changed overnight. But then she clears her throat, seeming to sense that an explanation is in order. "You are not being let go. Nor are you expected to work as a stewardess again aboard this boat."

"So—" I swallow, trying to process this. "So what do I do?"

Mrs. Colding spreads her hands slightly before clasping them once more. "That is entirely up to you, my dear."

I bark a weary laugh, shaking my head. "I don't know what's going on here."

Mrs. Colding's lips purse. "I don't think he knows either, if that's any comfort to you."

My heart stumbles in a little flutter.

Mrs. Colding sighs, regarding me. "If I were to give you any advice—if I were the sort of woman who gave advice—I would say to allow whatever happens to happen. Enjoy this for what it is—an honor. Do not think you are like the others; you are not. Understand? You are special, Aurora. It is a special thing, to be here." She hesitates, overcome with awkwardness, and tries a slight smile before turning to go.

There's a quaver in my voice that stops her at the door. "Mrs. Colding."

She turns, surprised. "Yes, dear?"

"Thank you."

She is not ready for this. She blinks, mouth twitching uncertainly, gratefully. "You're welcome," she says, and shuts the door.

I sit there and study the breakfast tray before me in the troughs of my undulating bedspread. When I lift the cover, steam wafts up and coils away to reveal a decadent feast that seems delivered from another world: avocado toast, savory rice porridge, yogurt, apple sauce, water and ginger ale on the side. Perfect for my food poisoning-ravaged stomach. I take in the VIP suite, the clothes, the sea beyond the windows. A view of the fabulously rich. I drag in a deep, steadying breath and let it out with puffed cheeks and rounded lips. Somewhere above, deckhands are calling out orders as they do a washdown. Far away, I can hear the cries of gulls.

SIXTEEN

I sleep for most of the day. At some point I wake to find a meal set out for me, a set of silver silk pajamas. I shower, letting the hot water pound on my shoulders, groaning like a drunk. Then collapse back into bed.

When I wake again it's dark. The digital clock by the bed reads 3 a.m. Jesus, I need some air.

I pad out in my silk pajamas into the passageway, rubbing at my eyes. The stern would be nice at this hour. I wonder, vaguely, in what part of the Mediterranean we are now. The fact that I no longer have to worry about my schedule is surreal. After nearly a week of having every second of my life regimented and controlled by Mrs. Colding, this sudden freedom is hard to trust, almost scary. Not unlike, I think, stepping free from my life with Josh.

I'm heading through the dining room to the aft doors when I hear the music.

I stop, listening. It's piano music. Slow, and stately, and hauntingly sad, drifting quietly through the sleeping yacht. It must be close.

And then I think of where a piano is on the *Lair*. And for whom that room is reserved.

I ascend winding stairs and pad through rooms made strange with night. I know I must stop, that this is a curiosity I should not indulge. But I don't. The music grows louder, its pained melancholy luring me helplessly on. Ahead, the door to the library stands ajar. A faint light from within.

I hesitate before it, head cocked, listening.

I'm trembling all over.

This is not like the pool. This entrancing music—there is something to it that is more private, angrily despairing. A deep and grievous wound. Something that should not be witnessed or shared. *(You must knock before entering.)*

But how could I interrupt this music, when it's the most beautiful thing I've ever heard?

I place my hand on the door, as if that would get me closer to that sound, and creak it wide.

The music instantly stops in a jarring of notes.

I stiffen, heart racing, but there is no one there. No tortured figure at the baby grand piano. Just the spines of books glowing dimly in the light of shaded lamps.

I stare, disbelieving, and step into the room. But there is no man lurking in any of the shadowed corners. No Voper, seething or aloofly embarrassed by my interruption. And there is no door connecting onto this room other than the one I entered. Where did he go?

At last I return to my suite, wondering if I'm now hearing things as well, if the side effect of my fever is wanting to see Voper everywhere I turn.

My fever breaks the next day. I grow more restless, pacing the cabin as my thoughts return, over and over again, to Voper. I can't get his smile out of my head, or the way he looked at me when he put his hand to my cheek. His tortured playing lingers in my ears.

What is happening to me? Why am I here? Why am I drawn to him?

But you know, Aurora, don't you? Pain seeks pain, after all. All it wants is to be understood.

As dusk falls, I slip out into the passageway and approach the antechamber at its end. The red doors of Voper's master suite loom huge and lurid in the dimness, as if beckoning.

Why? Why is his cabin forbidden? Why does only Mrs. Colding enter?

I place my ear to the doors.

Nothing. Lordly silence within. And then, suddenly, I hear it—a scuffling sound. A labored groan.

Panic jolts through me, the hairs at the back of my neck rising, and I dart away.

As night draws the shadows long in my cabin, I hold them both. In one hand, my phone with its barrage of Cailee's unanswered texts: *You're not hooking up with him, are you?* In the other, Voper's note and the knowledge of his interest: *Perhaps we'll bump into each other later, wandering the boat at some strange hour.*

I lower my phone.

I shower, shave my legs. The Hermès bags are waiting for me in the wardrobe. I lay out the clothes one by one on the bed, my jaw on the floor. I've never seen such clothing in my life, let alone touched it. I run my hands down the material, marveling. Dresses glitter and sparkle, beaded with sequins, a parade of glamour. But I don't go for those. They scream expectation, and I don't know what to expect tonight. So I choose something simple and elegant. I choose what Voper would wear, if he were a woman—a short black dress. It's not short enough to make me look like a high-class call girl, but I can't deny that it makes my waist look tiny and my ass amazing. The sheer tights I choose, however, gets me closer to call girl territory.

A little flush of satisfaction sweeps through me. It's not often that a runt like me feels powerful, and not merely cute. I choose a pair of black flats to go with the dress, and not harm the *Lair*'s teak decking. My hair is almost a stranger's, let down from its yachtie's ponytail to hang in dark, bold waves around my pale face. I know what will make that fair skin pop. I asked Mrs. Colding to retrieve my makeup bag from my old cabin earlier, and now I take out my trademark tube of lipstick and apply. It's a vicious, violent red, to match Voper's doors. Red as poison in a fairy tale. Red as blood.

I can't wait to see the look on Voper's face when he sees me. I'm not sure what I want to happen after that.

I know where to go this time. I know he'll be waiting for me. I head straight for the library, moving through the dark yacht with the certainty of a dreamer. The library door is again ajar, but no music comes from within. I lift my hand and knock.

The door creaks slightly inward, and I peek my head in. Empty. I bite my bottom lip.

This is foolishness.

Wandering the boat at night, hoping for—what? Has he plainly told you what he wants? Do you really know what's happening here?

I've turned to go when I hear it—a low creaking.

A bookshelf has moved. A bookshelf I'd thought flush with the wall has now cracked open like a door, for that is what it is.

A thought comes: *Turn back now. Don't do this*.

I put my hand on the bookshelf and part it further. It swings easily on unseen hinges, and without sound. Had it made a sound I might have turned back. But it doesn't.

There are metal steps, bright with white paint, conducting down behind the wall of bookshelves into darkness.

At the bottom of the stairwell, a corridor. And ahead, light. There is a room back there.

So it was true, then, what Mrs. Colding said. Secret rooms, secret places, hidden away on this boat. And I am going into one now, following a man who attracts me but brims with mystery.

This is what I can fall into.

The light brightens, and soon I emerge into an impossibly large room, its far wall a window set into the hull. It soars up perhaps twelve feet in height, twenty or more across. The waterline dances near its top, and I realize it's looking out into the deeps—an underwater observation lounge. Before it stands a man in a suit, hands in pockets, his body turned slightly in a bulky twist of muscle. The sight of him makes me pulse in all the sensitive parts of my body.

I'm about to open my mouth and speak when the unmistakable specter of a Great White glides out of the abyssal black toward the observation window, and the words fizzle on my lips. It's immense, as long as the window itself, all bulky, robust body and fearsome jaws of jagged, serrated teeth. But Voper does not recoil, does not give any indication of fear at all. He lifts his face to it, lifts a hand and touches the glass by its black and lifeless eye. My breath is caught in my throat. There is something not unlike the other, in that pale man and the pale man-eater. And then the moment is gone. The shark glides on, Voper drops his hand.

He speaks.

"You found me." He has not turned from the glass. He seems to regard his pale reflection.

"Yes." My voice, to my horror, comes out a little shaky.

I suddenly feel ridiculous, standing here in a tight black dress in the belly of a yacht at night.

And then Voper turns to look at me.

He goes very still, his face imperceptibly slackening. His eyes, so very blue in this light, trail down me head to toe, taking their time. Then they go back up, lingering on my legs, the hem of my dress, my face, my lips. His throat constricts in a swallow, and I realize this is the first time I have seen Adrian Voper, billionaire, at a loss for words.

My ankle wobbles.

He steps up to me, both hands in his pockets now, as if to restrain himself. His eyes drop to my blood-red lips. He seems lost in some private sensation, nostrils flared. And then he comes back to himself. His own full lips purse in a smirk. "You look"—he draws it out—"as if you've recovered."

I snort. *Well-played.* "I am. I have." Humiliating memories rush back to me and I put a hand to my brow. "Oh, God. I can't believe you saw all that . . ."

His mouth quirks. "It never happened, if that's what you'd prefer."

"Yes, *please*," I beg, laughing. "I very much prefer."

He waves a hand. "Forgotten, then."

We stare into each other's eyes, smiling. How can I not melt into a puddle in the presence of that smile? "Thank you, Mr. Voper."

"Adrian," he says. "Please."

"Adrian." It sounds so strange on my tongue. So normal. And at the same time an invitation to an exclusive, faraway place. A gift.

But the gifts, apparently, have just begun.

"I come here to think," he says, turning back to the window to watch a school of silvery fish flow past. "The quiet, you see. The stillness. The dark." He regards me. "What do you think of it?"

"It's beautiful," is my simple reply, because it's true.

He nods, pleased. "Come, then," he says, and holds out his arm in a courtly gesture. "I have something to show you."

SEVENTEEN

My mind races as he leads me through the quiet bowels of the *Lair*. I have no idea what he has in mind, even less so when we come out on the main deck and I see the limo tender bobbing against the swim platform with its fenders over the side, held in place by deckhands manning stern and bow lines, Jason at attention like a toy soldier. I scan the nighttime horizon—we're miles out at sea.

"Where on earth are we going?" I whisper.

But the reclusive billionaire beside me plays sphinx. "You'll see." He calls out expansively to Jason. "All set, Mr. Young?"

Jason nods, eyes widening at the sight of my dress before carefully avoiding me. "Double and triple-checked. Ready to go."

"Excellent." Voper *(Adrian)* offers me a hand to help me aboard, smoothly cutting Jason out of this step of yachting courtesy, and the first mate follows us aboard in silence. My cheeks grow warm at this show of territorial protectiveness. As Adrian guides me to the leather seat in back, I'm keenly aware of how my body looks in this dress. How I could barely board without showing my underwear. How all the men here are sneaking glances at me. As I cross my legs, the tights on my thighs rubbing softly together, I can't help but notice the red sniper-dot of Adrian's eyes on them. When I glance at him, he looks away and covers by glaring at Jason, who quickly breaks off a curiously serious appraisal of me. The lines are cast off, the deckhand behind the wheel carves an easy arc around to the side of the *Lair*, and I idly wonder if there will be a fight before we get to where we're going.

"Well?" I whisper to Adrian as spray mists my skin. "This boat can't take us anywhere out here."

"No," he concurs, and points. "But that can."

I lift my eyes, and my jaw drops.

A gull wing door is open near the bow of the *Lair*, and out of this foredeck locker a single-arm launching crane has swung out. Hanging from it is a canary-yellow, bubble-glassed submarine, revolving slowly as it's lowered into the ocean.

I splutter. "That's . . ."

"Yes," Adrian confirms.

"But . . . that's a submarine. You have a *submarine*."

"Submersible," he corrects, mouth crooking. "But yes."

The tender boat slows and Adrian, now on the foredeck at the bow, hops onto the submersible's swim platform, undogs the hatch wheel at the top of the glass bubble and hinges it open, all while in an impeccably tailored suit. It's somehow the sexiest thing I've ever seen.

Then he holds out a hand.

"*Me?*" I snort.

"You." He smiles, an enigmatic flicker of his lips. "You only live once."

I can't say no to that smile—but now I have to impress him. I slip off my flats, hand them to Jason, and jump onto the submersible beside Adrian, ignoring the offered hand. He smirks; mission accomplished. "After you," he says.

It's quite the trick to lower myself through the hatch in my short dress without flashing everyone, but I manage it. Just. Trying to calm my breathing, I take stock of my new surroundings. The cockpit is an acrylic sphere of glass bristling with consoles. I'm in one of two leather seats, and before I know it Adrian has lowered himself through the hatch into the other one. He screws the hatch tight and turns to me. His face is mere feet away and I am overwhelmed by his presence, the closeness of his body. It's going to be one hell of a ride.

"You okay?" he asks.

I nod, not trusting myself to speak, and he picks up a walkie-talkie. "Ready when you are, Mr. Young."

"Roger that," Jason's voice crackles back.

He hops onto the submersible—it's bobbing and rolling around on the sea's surface like a toy top—and begins to shrug off the harness on the submersible that's attached to the crane.

And there, crouched close by the glass sphere, he turns his head to look in at us.

No. Not us. *Me.*

He watches me with a strangely conflicted reluctance, and I feel a cold wash of foreboding shoot through me.

Then the harness is lifted away and Jason hops back onto the tender boat, radio to lips.

"You're ready to dive, Mr. Voper."

"Thank you, Mr. Young." Adrian eyes me. "Ready?"

Another breathless nod. He must see I'm crawling with nerves, because he speaks very steadily as he reaches down to turn a knob. "You're going to hear some air release. And there's going to be some pressure in your ears."

There's a hissing—the venting of the ballast—and the whole craft suddenly tips forward in a sickening lurch and I claw at Adrian's arm, feeling as if I'm about to fall out through the glass sphere. "Oh-my-fucking-God."

"It's okay," he says calmly. "It'll roll back in a minute."

That minute does not come nearly fast enough. Plumes of bubbles cloud out of the vents around us, and the water bobbing around the glass sphere we're in sloshes up and swallows us and the choppiness of the surface is replaced with a sudden calm. We're under.

"Holy shit," I breathe, craning my head up. The *Lair*'s lights dance above us, raying down into the depths. My 360-degree view from our bubble shows a cool blue twilight quickly fading to black. We're falling, imperceptibly but definitively descending toward the ocean floor, two beams of light blasting out from the submersible into the void. Even the thought of all that crushing weight on top of us cannot suppress the awe that is spreading through me. Far off, I see the shapes of dolphins flitting through the wavery murk.

"What is this?" I shiver.

But he does not answer me. He only smiles, and takes hold of the fighter jet-style joystick between us. The submersible glides about, and suddenly its twin beams of light travel over a coral reef, an astonishing explosion of color that takes the breath out of me. Fish and moray eels dart in and out of fantastic growths, hot vents blur and ripple water. But this glimpse of a luminous undersea kingdom is soon, in turn, gone. We drop lower, the water shading bluer and bluer, then black. The *Lair*'s lights above us are long gone. We are a speck in the void, the only thing seen the twin beams before us, motes of detritus drifting through them.

And it hits me: I am trapped alone at the bottom of the sea with Adrian Voper.

His proximity is like a drug. We're so close we're sharing the same breath, this space so cramped our knees are touching. I make a mental note to add knees to my list of erogenous zones.

When Adrian turns to me, his pale face is very serious. "Do you trust me?"

I moisten my lips. It trembles out of me: "Yes."

He smiles, a seam of white teeth that makes me feel giddily, inexpressibly flattered.

Then he flicks a switch and we're plunged into pitch black.

I suck in a breath, rocketed into sudden terror. I am hyperventilating. My body is screaming for light, for release, for blasting up to the surface and into the pure air of the world above.

Adrian shifts in the dark, places a hand on the warm fat of my thigh. *Wait.*

And then I see it.

A light streaks by like a star, so sudden it jolts me. Then another. A bioluminescent particle, a streamer of electric blue light.

Very slowly, very calmly, Adrian begins to speak.

"I've found it is good for me to come down here," he says. "As a reminder." More lights outside our bubble now: fizzing rocket ships, explosions of sparks, squirts of what looks like eerie blue smoke. "Creatures of the dark—they reveal themselves to you in their own time." Alien forms glide out of the abyss. Things that are nothing but luminous lures and bobbing mouths of hideous recurved fangs. Long ganglions of siphonophores that look like feather boas of purple and pink light. Shrimps that spew clouds of blue luminescence out of their mouths like fire-breathing dragons. "And when that happens—when you are lucky enough to see that happen—you are quite frequently overwhelmed by their beauty." A jellyfish flashes a hypnotic, rotating pinwheel pattern around its body. Strange shapes pulse with yellow-green rows of bioluminescent organs. A structure of light, longer than a giant squid, trails by in a stately constellation of luminescence like an undersea galleon.

It is a light show, a fireworks show that rivals anything above water. It is overwhelming. Exhilarating. I am dizzy with awe.

But my skin prickles, the hairs on my arms have raised because of the person beside me. Because of what is happening.

Adrian Voper is trying to tell me something.

"They are underseen," he continues. "Misunderstood. And for that reason they can be feared, or shunned." He falls into silence and I do not turn to look at him, afraid he will stop talking, that the transformation that is occurring will cease as abruptly as it began. But he doesn't. "It can be a lonely thing," he adds at last, his voice low, "to live in the dark."

And he reaches out, his cool hand slipping into mine, fingers entwining. A magical event, a shimmering touch that gives me goosebumps all over. What is happening to me? I am plumped up with self-esteem, rewarded and sweetly assured. I am packed full of happiness.

I have been given Adrian Voper's secrets, here at the bottom of the world.

EIGHTEEN

The return to the *Lair* is a blur. I barely notice the submersible's ascent, a brooding Jason taxiing us back to the swim platform. I am swept along in a dream as Adrian Voper escorts me to my cabin, the touch of his hand on the small of my back setting off in me a procession of sparks and chills.

I turn to face him at the door, my flats dangling from one hand. I am a mess of anticipation.

Does he know what I'm thinking? My mind is a deviant. I think of him pushing me inside and undressing me, trailing kisses down my neck, shoulders, breasts. Being seen, and honored, and set aglow.

What am I to do with myself? What will he do?

His expression melts into a slow smile as he watches me. "How was your night?"

I can barely speak. I drink in his vivid blue eyes, his satirical mouth, his slick but brambly hair. I want to run my hands through that hair. I want . . .

"It was . . . something," I respond at last. We both laugh, and my voice lowers, becomes solemn. "It made me think of . . ."

"What?"

"Well . . . my name."

"Your name?"

"Yeah. My father, he proposed to my mother under the Northern Lights. And so they named me after them."

He smiles, amused. "Aurora." God, I love hearing my name in his mouth.

"Yeah." I go on before I can stop myself. "Those lights down there reminded me of them. I've always dreamt of seeing them one day." I laugh, a glassy little sound. "I've never told anyone that."

"Well," he murmurs, his eyes fixed on mine. "I'm glad you felt you could."

"Me too," I barely manage back.

A silence falls between us. His eyes drop to my lips, and I bite them. His eyes trail down my skin, and I press my knees together.

I can feel the warmth spreading to my cheeks. I drop my eyes, smiling to myself, sparkling with stupid hope.

I know what's next.

But the moment passes; he makes no move. He studies me with a strange, reserved expression that's somehow pained, as if I'm a torment to him. What was I thinking?

You'll never do better than me, Josh's voice taunts.

"Well," I blurt shakily, lifting my flats, and his face changes. "Thanks for a special night." I turn hurriedly away—

And then his hand is gripping my arm, whirling me back to him, and our teeth click as our lips come together.

It's so sudden it takes me a moment to process what's happened. Our eyes are wide open, and we regard each other warily as always. There's a faint bite, his teeth pull at my bottom lip and let go, and chills spread. My nipples perk. My toes curl into the carpet. My tongue checks for blood, but he was too soft, too careful for that. His lashes lower, and he leans in again. My mind reels, desperate for answers, and it's only when his mouth slides against mine, gently, intoxicatingly urging it open, that it hits me.

He's kissing me. Adrian Voper. Adrian. Kissing me.

My flats drop from nerveless fingers to the floor. I'm frozen, entranced. For a moment, I'm at a loss as to what to do. But Adrian isn't; far from it. His lips teach me. *This is what it's really like to be kissed*, they say. *This is what it's like to be kissed by a man who wants you.*

Let it happen. Drink me in. Let me lick you, bite you, possess you.

Okay.

I grip the lapels of his suit, pulling him close as I arc into him, filling myself with his scent. He smells of dead flowers, tastes like the cold, sweet air in a well, sharp and clean. God, I've never been kissed like this before. This is nothing like the clumsy declarations of need from the farm boys in Oregon. Nothing like Josh. This—this is decadent. It's as if I'm some dessert melting in the sun that he's licking up, and he doesn't want to waste a drop. I'm a rarity. I'm being discovered. I have become his world.

How could I ever want this to end?

But it does. When he pulls away to look in my eyes I sway after him, drunk with sensation, lips still parted. I let out a little indignant sound of frustration and loss, and his eyes glint with amusement. He dips his head, lips grazing my ear, down my neck, breathing me in, and I shiver. Pale fingers glide down me, tracing quivering arteries, the hollow of my throat, the swell of my breasts in my dress, and he sighs. His body is pressed against mine, and everywhere we touch I grow warm. I wait, breath held, aching for what's next. I am overcome with a rush of helplessness, a sinking yielding that leaves me limp. What has he done to me?

Then he's gone. His fine fingers curl away, as if restraining themselves. He draws back, his dark eyes returning to their normal, vivid blue, cleared of a fervent hunger. He smiles a sharp smile. "I didn't want you to think I was uninterested."

"Oh," I wheeze, struggling in vain to regain the ability of speech. "Yeah. That was, uh . . . yeah. Mission accomplished."

His eyes crinkle. "Good night, Aurora," he says, and flows like liquid shadow down the passageway. Gone.

When I shut the cabin door and lean against it, I can't help it—I jump up and down in a little dance of glee, pumping my fists in the air like a crazy woman.

So this is life. Crackling with possibility, bursting at the seams with happiness.

I could get used to this.

There's a polite rap on the door, and I instantly default to ground-based normalcy. Clearing my throat and finger-combing my hair, I open the door, expecting to see an amused Adrian Voper, eyes bright with a change in plans.

But I don't. It's Jason, looking jumpy, unsure, concerned. "Hey," he says.

"Hellooo," I caution. "What's up?"

He glances in the direction of Adrian's suite. "I, uh, wanted to tell you something."

"Okay."

I've never seen him like this. He looks pale, almost frightened. He runs a hand through his sandy hair. "Look, it isn't easy to tell you this. But I wanted to warn you—"

"Warn me?"

"Yeah. Voper, he—you shouldn't see him—"

I place a hand on my hip, brow arched. "I think I can make that decision for myself, thanks."

He huffs out a breath, nods, a guilty, dorky grin spreading across his face. "Right. Of course. I just think you should know everything before making that decision."

I try to sense what's behind all this, this aggressive, presumptuous persistence—and it clicks. "Look, Jason," I sigh. "I like you, okay? But you had your chance—"

"No, that's not—" He raises his hands, eyes squinched shut, and takes a breath. "Look. You don't know him. He's dangerous—"

"*Dangerous?*" I roll my eyes. "Okay, that's enough. I'm done. Goodnight, Jason." I begin to shut the door.

"Arie, please—"

"Good*night*, Jason." Click. I growl out a groan deep in my throat, head thrown back. Why can't I just enjoy this moment?

I fall back on the bed and reach for my phone to call Cailee. Celebration time.

Her sleepy voice answers on the seventh ring. "Arie? You do know it's, like, six in the morning, right?"

"Yes, but you *have* to hear what just happened!" I squeal, and I can all but see Cailee sit up in bed, brow furrowed. "What do you mean?"

"He took me on a date."

A groan.

"No, listen. He took me on a ride in a submersible. At *night*. It was *amazing*—"

"A *submersible?*"

"I know, right?! And then he kissed me. Oh my *God*—"

"Jesus. Is this why I haven't heard from you in days?"

"No, that was Emmie poisoning me—"

"Emmie *what?*"

"Don't worry. Adrian booted her off the boat."

"*Adrian?* He's *Adrian* now?" She sounds like she has her face in her hands. "Girl, I hope you know what you're doing."

"I do. He's not—"

"An asshole?"

"Well . . ."

"Yup."

"Okay, he's intense. But he's not like that. It's like . . . there's something driving him to be that way . . ."

"Uh-huh." Cailee has an infuriating ability to vocalize her eyes rolling. "Never heard *that* one before."

"Okay, I know how it sounds. But he's a good guy. There's just . . . something going on underneath. He was trying to tell me tonight . . ."

"You mean when he wasn't trying to show you how rich he is?"

My turn to roll my eyes. "Ha ha. Very funny. You can shut up now."

"Just sayin'," she snorts. "Sounds like someone's been enjoying herself . . ."

"Shut *up!*" I whine, pounding the bed with a fist, and she breaks down in a peal of laughter. When she finally recovers, there's a wheedling tone in her voice. "I just want you to be careful, okay babe?"

"I know." Then, a slow grin creeping up my face, "Did I tell you about the clothes he got me?"

I pose with them later, holding them over my body in front of the mirror. One slinky, shimmering outfit after another. It's only when I dip into the bottom of the last bag that I find the several sets of lingerie. My jaw drops. They're gorgeous—lacy confections in black and red, sheer and slashed into sensuous designs.

Babydolls, bustiers, submissive strappy bralettes. A black lace harness teddy with garters catches my eye. The very sight of it makes me blush. I chew a nail, picturing myself in it.

Screw it.

I shimmy out of my clothes and into the teddy, cock a hip and inspect myself. It looks even better than I thought it would—I look like a goddamn sex goddess. My breasts are cupped up and bouncy, my hips shapely, the outfit's black lace diving into a coy triangle between my legs. I wonder if he thought of me in this when he chose it. What I would look like. What he would do to me.

My throat is suddenly dry.

I lie on the bed in the teddy, luxuriating in the rapturous feel of its fabric, its fit, its intimate conforming to my body. As if it was somehow him conforming to me—him holding me. For so long, Josh had made me feel invisible, desexualized, my desires something to be ashamed of. But Adrian . . .

My belly rises and falls heavily, unevenly. I'm tremoring with nerves, a warm tingling between my legs. I glide a hand down the lace, thinking of his hands on me. The way he caught my lip in his teeth, blazing me to life. I have that to think of, as my fingers glide lower, dipping beneath. That and the dizzying power of his mouth. His indismissible dark eyes.

NINETEEN

The note is waiting for me in the morning: *Guests at 8:00 tonight. Care to accompany me?*

My heart does a little squee.

The day can't pass quickly enough. I spend it pacing my cabin, doing yoga on the sun deck, sitting with my knees hugged to chest before the sheet of glass in the underwater observation lounge, watching dolphins cavort past and thinking of secrets given up in darkness.

I don't see Adrian Voper once all day.

At six I start getting ready. Absurdly, ridiculously, I want to impress his friends, and so I choose something that's a little more flashy for tonight: a gauzy, high-slit champagne dress that lets one leg strut out and my breasts hang like delicious pearls beneath plunging halter ribbons. When I finish it off with earrings winking out of my mane of hair and my bright-red lipstick that hardens the shape of my mouth, I don't even recognize myself.

Dusk is falling when I step out onto the aft main deck to watch the other yacht arrive. It seems the whole crew is on deck; they've been talking about nothing else all day. I try my best to ignore all the looks I get, the whispers behind cupped hands. Captain Redfearn does not seem to know what to make of me. Jason, at his post by the stern lines, eyes me unhappily.

A voice whispers in my ear. "Ignore them."

I turn to see Mrs. Colding, hands clasped before her, as courteous as ever. But the air is different between us. It's confiding, conspiratorial. Almost friendly. She leans in and adds in a wry tone, "Yachties thrive off gossip."

I smirk. It's true.

And her saying this allows me, finally, to ignore my own doubts and feel it: the pride in knowing I am the woman who will be on Adrian's arm. That somehow this floating pleasure palace has become half mine.

The feeling sweeps through me, buoying me up, until the breath catches in my throat.

It takes a moment for me to follow what Mrs. Colding says next. "That one's been moody all day." She juts her chin at Jason, her eyes lingering on me knowingly. "He's been taking it out on the deckhands, making them polish and wax the hand rails the entire afternoon."

I study Jason again, the smallest twinge of guilt nagging at me. It must suck being in his shoes right now.

I shake this off, focusing my gaze on our surroundings. We've anchored in a private bay somewhere along the Corsican coast, and the sea is burnished red by the boiling demise of the sun. It is out of this lurid glare that the other yacht glides.

She's almost as big as the *Lair*, her bulky hull cutting through the water like a shark. Also like the *Lair*, her windows are darkly tinted, her design private, discreet. She slowly circles us, and I catch a glimpse of the name backlit in blue on her transom: *Vespertine*. Then she slows, stops. There's the splash of her anchor, the rattling of her chain, and silence.

Minutes later, the *second* yacht arrives.

Seriously? This one's smaller, elegant, but no less magnificent, and similarly tinted. The name on her transom: *Lazaret*. She casts anchor on the other side of the *Lair*, and silence falls again.

What are they waiting for?

With a last flare of crimson the sun slips away, the lights of the three yachts glittering on the dark waters, and I hear a faint thump above me.

I step forward and crane my head up.

It's Jason. He's hopped over the rail and edged out in his bare feet onto the curving fiberglass stern of the deck above. As I watch, he unloops the halyard and lowers the courtesy flag (in this case, the flag of France), as is tradition at sunset. But he's not done—he's running up another flag to take its place. It slowly unfurls in the wind, a triangular black field on which ripple two inverted white triangles, glowing in the *Lair*'s uplights. Some kind of ensign for a yachting association.

Murmurs spread among the crew, and I turn to see the same pennant being hoisted in answer on the *Vespertine* and *Lazaret*.

What is going on?

I'm still standing there watching, befuddled, when full night descends on the bay and there's a soft footfall behind me.

Goosebumps break out on my arms; I already know who it is before I turn. Onto the aft deck flows Adrian Voper in a black gala tux, his hair slicked back in a gleaming wave. He looks impossibly handsome.

And he's staring at me as if he's never seen a woman before.

Mrs. Colding, mouth twitching, smoothly excuses herself.

All eyes are on us as he comes up to me. But I tune out everything. The looks, the whispers, Jason's sullen expression as he reappears on the aft deck. I lift my chin. "Hi," I say as Adrian steps close. Like a dolt, I'm furiously blushing.

"Hi." His eyes rove over me, and I feel ransacked with happiness. The memory of our kiss hovers between us like a tangible thing. "How is it that you look even more amazing than you did last night?"

Jesus, compliments look good on him.

I scramble for a reply, but am spared by everyone's attention shifting to the water. Limousine tenders are gliding out from the *Vespertine* and *Lazaret*, ferrying over tonight's guests. I take the opportunity to change the subject. "Who are your friends?"

Adrian's jaw tenses at the question. He grits out with an airy coolness, "Business associates."

"So you're entertaining tonight."

He snorts, hands in pockets now. "Something like that." He turns to me, his eyes all glittery black. "I want you to know, I'm going to have to be . . . a little different tonight. In front of them."

"You mean a brooding asshole?"

He laughs, a sudden, unguarded bark of happiness, and my heart glows like a thousand-watt lightbulb. "Yes. That."

"Is that so different from what you usually are?"

"It is," he says, nodding, very serious. "It does feel different since I met you."

It's suddenly hard to breathe. I don't know what to say to that.

Adrian looks out at the tender boats coasting up to the swim platform. Their occupants: two men in elegant suits, the *Lair*'s lights shining on pale foreheads, pale skin. On their arms, women in shimmery club dresses.

Adrian swallows, great packs of muscle clenched hard under his coat, and the penny drops: *He's nervous.*

I do it before I've even thought about it—I take his hand. "Hey. It'll be okay."

He looks down at the hand, at me, and his expression eases into something like gratitude. He smiles. "Okay."

TWENTY

When both of the limousine tenders have glided up alongside the swim platform, one of the men calls out with mock formality. "May we come aboard?"

He's staring, right past Captain Redfearn, at Adrian.

The captain scowls. Adrian forces a smile and gestures. "Please."

The businessmen are, in a word, strange. The owner of the *Lazaret* is an Italian, chic and cadaverous-looking, with a dainty mien. The owner of the *Vespertine* is a hollow-cheeked Easterner with a broad forehead and the kind of probing humor that's edged with malice. I've known men like him before. The first time he looks at me, I get a chill.

"Aurora, this is Signore Spalatro and Anatoly Anatolovich," Adrian says. "Very old friends."

It happens before I know it: Anatoly bends and with stiff courtliness bestows a kiss on the back of my hand. "Charmed."

My hand is trembling when he lets it go.

Adrian clenches his jaw and turns to the women, who are studying me head to toe with contemptuous sloe eyes like glittering, predatory creatures, but neither of the businessmen move to introduce them. "Well?" Anatoly prompts, raising his eyebrows.

Wow.

Mrs. Colding steps forward with a smile. "This way, gentlemen."

As the men are led away, I fall in step with the glamazons. I'm preparing a peace offering in my head when the tallest of them quips out of the corner of her mouth, "Welcome to the sugar babe parade."

"What?" I splutter, feeling the blood rush to my face. "Oh, no, I'm not—"

"I'm rather new to the whole yachtsman sex toy thing," says my new best friend, flicking painted nails. "But . . . does your guy *always* send you back to your suite after fuck time? Like, I never *actually* sleep in the same bed as him."

One of Spalatro's girls chimes in. "And what's with the suits, and always staying inside?"

I still at that. "Always?"

The girls nod. "I mean, it's like they think they'll burst into flames if they go out in the sun. Why bother owning a yacht if you can't even enjoy it?"

As the models gossip away—"I'd watch that one . . . Anatoly? He likes ordering obscure cocktails so he can fire the stewardesses who can't prepare them"—I watch Adrian's back as he glides inside the *Lair*, my neck prickling. It's the feeling of something concealed from me—all around me, but concealed—something I cannot guess at. Not dark with malevolence: a silly, tiresome, harmless little secret, surely. If anything at all.

What childish thoughts I am having.

We retire to the entertainment lounge with its plush leather seats and dazzling chandelier. The businessmen glide about in suits that shine like sharkskin, sinking onto sofas in lordly laziness. The women dutifully drape themselves over them as Adrian and I settle into armchairs beside each other, fingers brushing. I feel a reassuring crackle of electricity at our touch.

It doesn't last long.

"My dear Voper," Anatoly opens in a thick but refined accent, "whatever happened to your parade of blonde supermodels?" His haughty eyes alight on me before dropping to Adrian's fingers all but joined with mine, and Adrian's hand retreats into a clenched fist on the armrest of his chair.

Oh.

"People change," Adrian says stiffly, and Anatoly's lips seam back in a smile. His teeth, I note, are yellow, and very long.

"Do they?" he croons, and exchanges a smirk with Spalatro. "Well. Taste does, apparently."

My heart is hammering as Thea and Mrs. Colding sweep in for cocktail orders. Thea gives me a hard, speculative look, and I shift my crossed legs, fighting a hot flush of shame. How ridiculous I must look in this shimmering gown, these earrings, this lipstick. A country rube playing dress-up with the adults.

The orders blur in my ears—"A Hangman's Blood", Anatoly sweetly purrs—and I wave off mine, my stomach revolting at the thought of alcohol. The stews withdraw behind the marble bartop, and Anatoly resumes his fun.

"The Commodore sends his greetings." His voice is low and cool. A cat playing with a mouse. "He's missed you."

Adrian's voice, in turn, is hard as granite. "I've been busy."

Spalatro regards me with faint amusement, one long, pale hand resting on a bare thigh beside him. "We see that."

My cheeks grow hot. There is a tension here, some old wound these two pasty parasites obviously delight in reopening, but I don't care to learn the details at the moment. My head is roaring, my shoulders trembling with suppressed anger. So when attention turns to a kerfuffle behind the bar, I seize the opportunity for an escape.

"Be right back," I promise and saunter away, not waiting for Adrian to respond. His eyes are down, his hands fisted, and despite my anger I feel a pang of sympathy for him.

Thea and Mrs. Colding look up from their hushed conference as I approach. "What is it?" I whisper, and they glance at each other. Thea is pale and trembling.

"His drink," she mumbles. "Anatoly's. I can't remember the recipe. It's not in the mixology book, and the wifi is shit right now." She waves her phone, voice rising in a frazzled panic. "If I can't give him what he wants—"

"Okay, okay. Here. Let me." I scoot past behind the bar, switching smoothly into bartending mode. A calmness settles in me as muscle memory flows back into my hands, and I start grabbing bottles.

"How do you know this?" Mrs. Colding hisses.

I shrug. "I was always doing exotic cocktails to impress my friends, back when I tended bar. I'm . . . not great at small talk, so this was how I could socialize. By doing something." I swallow back a flood of self-consciousness, glance over to see Adrian is watching me, having heard every word, and shake a lock of hair out of my face. "Anyway. This one's double measures of gin, whiskey, rum, port and brandy." I slide open the back bar cooler and peer at the selection of beers nestled in chips of ice. "Do you have a stout beer?"

Another exchanged look. "I can get one from the beach club bar," Thea offers.

The stout's added, and I top it up with champagne. The end result is a dangerously dark-looking concoction. Thea deflates in teary relief, runs a hand through her hair, sniffles—and crushes me in a hug. "Thank you," she whispers fiercely, and pulls back. "I'm sorry if—if I've been a dick since—"

"No, really, it's okay," I smile. "Just—let me do the honors?"

She nods, and there's a small, admiring smirk on Mrs. Colding's face as I turn and march up to the waiting guests. They've all been watching this scene with undisguised interest, eyebrows raised. I hold out the drink to Anatoly like a coronation tribute. "I hope it's to your . . . *taste*, Anatoly Anatolovich."

The Easterner's lips curl in amusement. Adrian glows with blatant pride. The jaw of Anatoly's sex toy hangs.

Anatoly takes a small evaluative sip, eyes never leaving me, and smiles. "My, my," he breathes. "She's a hotblooded one, isn't she?" He flicks a look at Adrian. "Perhaps she should join us below?"

But Adrian's face slackens at this, as if devastated by some dire news. "I thought we weren't retiring to the staterooms until later—"

There's a malicious gleam in Anatoly's eye as he shrugs. "Why wait for the fun to start?"

What fun? What the hell are they talking about?

But Adrian, it seems, is fine with excluding me. He shakes his head. "I think not."

A small, hard hurt throbs in my chest, but I ignore it. "Actually, I'd like to—"

"No."

The cold finality in his voice turns heads, but Adrian carefully avoids everyone's gaze, sitting white-knuckled in his chair. He is cool, composed, deliberate. "You've had a long day," he explains with no feeling whatsoever. "You need your sleep."

My stomach folds in half. "Adrian, what is—"

"*What did I just say?*"

The ferocity leaves the room humming with a deadly silence. The businessmen look between Adrian and I with sly interest and suspicion. The women stare—unsure, jealous, gleeful.

Then Adrian stands, buttoning his coat over his lean, muscled frame. "Shall we?" And he turns away.

All glide after, Anatoly giving me one last, intrigued appraisal, the girls' perfect faces contorted in scorn. As they head for the cabins, one of them trails painted nails down Adrian's back.

To think, I looked good tonight.

A touch on my shoulder—Mrs. Colding, perhaps Thea—but I flinch away. I need to get out. I need air. I stumble out onto the aft deck and breathe in the night, the moon huge and glowy above me. I grip the rails to fight the feeling of my life falling backwards—back to a time when Josh would avoid admitting to others I was his girlfriend. When my feelings were framed as a burden. When he would cross a room as I huddled in the corner and snap at me, "Pull yourself together," as if he hadn't been the one, all along, to pull me apart.

You'll never do better than me.

No. That's not him. That's not Adrian. I know him better than that. There's something else going on here.

To hell with this.

I pound down stairs and passageways to the cabins on the main deck. Slipping off my flats, I tiptoe—a soft-footed and determined voyeur—to the red-stained doors of Voper's suite. The sight, unaccountably, stops me cold. Something is happening to me. A raising of the hairs on my arms, a tightening in the throat, that tells me I am in the grip of a swift and unreasonable suspicion.

But of what, I don't know.

I do know, though. I do know. It's the dread of the witness, the feeling that I am about to see something I will never be able to unsee.

No. Push this aside. This has no use for you right now.

So I take the step forward. I raise my hand, and do what I must do: I open the door to the room that must not be entered.

TWENTY-ONE

Adrian Voper's suite is impossibly immense, with no windows to be seen in that gloom. The redness of the doors continues inside: brutally expressionistic red canvases on the walls, vases of roses, an enormous bed with crimson silk covers. Those covers are all tangled up. Tangled up and moving.

For there are bodies in the bed. Pasty white forms that must be the businessmen, their flesh slightly loose and sagging on the bone, flesh that hasn't seen the light of day in years. They are bent over the women, whose heads are flung back and twisted to the side, as if struck down by some natural disaster. They hold them down, the men, long fingers splayed wide as bat wings over innocent-looking mounds of breasts, and place their mouths to young skin. From my crack in the door, it can't be seen what they're doing, but whatever it is must be effective—legs slowly writhe in the sheets, accompanied by low, delirious moans. There is the sound of sucking, like a kitten lapping cream.

Suddenly, Adrian Voper's dark eye is blinking back at me through the crack in the door.

I don't even have time to jump in fright. Before I know it, he's through the door and it's shut fast behind him. He is, I note, fully clothed. "What are you doing?" he snarls. "Only Mrs. Colding is allowed in here. Why aren't you in your room?"

I open my mouth to speak—but nothing comes out. He's quite a sight when he's like this: all glittery black eyes and a tensing jaw, his perfect posture pronounced by shoulder muscles ridged up in anger. His terrifying exquisiteness makes me swallow.

"What is that?" I get out at last. "Is that—is that an *orgy?*"

The words make him pale, if he actually could. He runs a hand down his face. "Look, I—"

But my fury blazes up again. "What is this? What kind of fucking business meeting is that? Why did you tell me—"

"I'm sorry, Aurora. I was trying to protect you. Those—" He glances back and lowers his voice. "Those are not good men, okay? I did not want you in that room."

I shift my weight, sullen and vulnerable. "Were you—were you *participating—*"

"*No!* No. This is—this is what's required, when I host them. This is how it is, for . . . what I do."

"And what is that, *exactly?* What *do* you do, Mr. Voper?"

He looks at me for a long, considering moment, shakes his head. "I can't tell you that."

"Why?"

"I just can't."

"*Why?*" I shout.

"*BECAUSE I CARE ABOUT YOU!*" The force of the explosion leaves us both speechless and breathing hard, inches from each other. Our eyes lock. He looks as stunned as I am. A thrilling tension grows, winding tighter and tighter, threatening to snap. I'm reminded of the way he looked when he rose out of the pool, huge and hulking and simmering of danger, and it crackles through me like an electric charge.

We. Are about. To fuck.

It happens faster than I can blink. He scoops me up by my ass and we crash against the wall, no doubt spiderwebbing it with cracks. My flats drop to the floor. My hands fall to his shoulders and my dress rides up my thighs. The breath has gone out of me in a whuff, but I don't care—because he's kissing me. And not like before. This is rough, ravenous, savage but tender. I push at his extravagantly muscled chest as if bracing on a rollercoaster. He does not budge. He is a brick wall, holding me in place. He vibrates with power, so intense it makes me feel limp and warm, blazing with sensitivity. When he pulls away, I come up for air as if surfacing into a strange atmosphere. His face is very close, he stares into my eyes. His voice comes out as a husky, angry promise. "No one's ever going to hurt you again, Aurora."

I shiver. No one—*no one*—uses my full name but him. And he knows it.

But how did he know? How did he know I'd been hurt before?

"I know you," he says, as if reading my thoughts. "I know pain when I see it." My heart thrums. "And I know what you want."

Goose bumps break out all over me—whoo daddy, yes, he does. I growl in impatience and grip the scruff of his hair, pulling him back. Like a good boy, he accommodates. His mouth is eating me, his white teeth sharp. He tugs furiously at my dress and I hear material tear; he's ripping my champagne gown to rags, fulfilling every woman's deepest fantasy. I hear the clink of his belt, and I can't help it—I moan, embarrassingly loud, thinking of what's coming next. And it does. A sudden, urgent pressure that surges inside me, bouncing me up against the wall. I clap a hand to my mouth to muffle my scream. I'd been expecting his size, given how much bigger he is than me—but *holy shit*. He begins to move with excruciating control, grinding up into me in a slick rolling of his hips, bouncing me up and down with every thrust. My hands claw at his shoulders, his neck, his hair. I wrap my legs around him. I can barely blink, barely breathe. This is the hottest moment of my life. All I had ever gotten from Josh was a cold, unwelcoming bed, a disinterest in intimacy. But this—I don't know how I can go back from this. I have never been taken like this before, *ravaged* like this before. He tangles his hands in mine and pins them against the wall above my head, presses his brow to mine, noses touching, and stares into my eyes. The passion there is so stark and real it sends wild terror bolting through me. How can I keep my composure in the face of that stare, ignore the sudden tightening of emotion in my chest, when I know that he wants nothing less than for me to hand over everything I am and ever have been, and be his?

It is too much. The pleasure cascades, and I am moaning and whimpering like a little puppy, lost in the extravagant torture of it. *Please, please.* I clutch at him, babbling pleas and brutal promises, my body helplessly quivering until I'm carried over a cliff into rushing darkness, annihilating oblivion.

Until I am sent—as if in sudden, blinding flight—over the edge.

The pleasure is searing, unbearable. I buck and claw and cry out, and he clamps a hand over my mouth as the waves of ecstasy ripple through me in a long subsiding spasm, leaving me wrung out, exhausted, on the far shore of where I once had been, who I once had been.

So. This is what they talk about. This is what we are capable of.

My eyes roll back in my head and I sag in sudden, heavy deliriousness, spent and empty as air. And he's joining me here, in this bright new world. His thrusting pleasure carrying him over to a complete abandon in which he shudders and groans and I cling to his neck, kissing and moaning into his mouth—"Come for me, baby, come for me"—and then he's exploding inside me in a flurry of amazed curses and I hold him to me, his head between my breasts, my hands in his hair, whispering, *shh*. I am swimming in a broth of devotion.

After a long time he sets me down, my ass sliding down the wall until I'm on my own quivering legs again. I suck in a big lungful of air and laugh. "Wow."

But he doesn't say anything.

"Adrian?" I turn to him. "What's wrong?"

He has his eyes squeezed shut, head down, one hand braced on the wall beside me. He is shivering as if with fever. A chill touches me, and I put a hand to his cheek. "Adrian?"

He chances a look at me, my skin flushed with color, and jerks away in a grimace of agony. His shoulders heave, he shakes his head. "I'm sorry," he says, his normally smooth voice rough with regret. "This was a mistake."

The bottom of my stomach drops out. "*What?*"

He looks at me with eyes hazed black, and the cold ferocity there makes my scalp crawl. When he opens his mouth again, it's sharp. "I made a promise: No one will ever hurt you again."

And he strides on down the passageway. Just like that. Gone.

I blink in place, look down at myself with burning cheeks and tug at my torn dress. I'm hard-used between the legs, swollen and stinging. How can the procedures of love turn, at a moment's notice, into the most shameful of things?

Shameful, yes. Such well-deserved shame.

To think that I'd fallen for another man who'd do that to me.

I start for my suite in a daze. The next step is clear: I will pack my bags, get off at the next port. Fly back to Cailee, or stay here in the Mediterranean and get hired on another boat. Have another life, without this man.

No.

I halt before the door to my suite, trembling. That will not be my story. Not again. I deserve answers, and I will get them. I march down the passageway, swept along on a tide of certainty. This confusion will be cleared up, this story reverted back to where it should be.

For is that not what love is? What it has always been?

A capturing tide, sweeping all before it. To happiness or ruin.

Let it be happiness.

I find him on the portside gangway, a darkly handsome silhouette against the bone whiteness of the teak decking. My call to him lodges in my throat when I realize: That shape is not one, but two people. For Thea is there, with her back to me. She seems to be embracing Adrian. No. Not embracing. At least, that is no normal embrace. She is swept up, twitching and bare toes grazing the deck, in Adrian's white hands gripping her by the shoulders. He seems to fold himself over her, his face burrowed in her neck, as if feeding on her. For that is what he is doing. He has crafted two long foreteeth into her neck and is drinking her blood.

When he looks up at me, those gorgeous blue-black eyes rolling up from under his brow to show the lower half of his face is bearded in gore, it is as if all the air has been sucked out of the sky.

Adrian. My Adrian. Drinking the blood of women.

This is the destruction: the sentence forms in my mind. *This is the destruction of your life*.

Thea's corpse drops from Adrian Voper's long, talon-like hands—*thump*—and I'm trying to scream but there's a stuttering of his pale shape toward me . . . and darkness.

TWENTY-TWO

I wake in utter darkness. My skull is pounding, and when I touch it my fingers come away damp. That's when I remember: Adrian Voper. Out on the teak decking. Flowing toward me like a pale nightmare.

"Hello, Aurora," comes his cool voice out of the darkness, and I shriek and scramble back against what must be a bed's headboard. I'm suddenly trembling all over. My heart wants to pound out of my chest. "Get away—get away from me!" I shriek into the pitch black, sobs catching in my throat, and I have to clutch at my head, whimpering at the pain.

His voice is heavy, and full of regret. "I apologize I had to resort to that. I could not risk your screams alerting anyone."

But Thea. But Thea.

I lurch away and fall out of bed, onto the floor. I can't even see my hands in front of my face, such is the purity of the darkness in this space. I grope along the wall and away from that voice, my chest ragged with pants. The door. There must be a door. The thought flies through my mind like a bird going to and fro in wild and marveling terror. *Get out. Get away.*

"Aurora. Please." A deep sadness in his voice now. "We need to talk."

And there. A doorknob. But it won't turn. The door won't open.

"Help—*help!*" I scream. "Mrs. Colding! Jason! *Help me!*"

"This room is soundproof." The explanation is calm, quiet, full of displeasure at that last name. "No one can hear you."

So. I am trapped here. In the dark. With the murderer of my friend.

I sink down against the door, weeping. There it is. The fact has hardened, has taken on its undeniable shape: Who I have loved. What I have loved. There is no going back from this, no turning away. Say to yourself, You did not know. Say to yourself, Anybody could have been taken in.

Unless it takes a certain kind of fool. A certain kind of foolish woman to believe there was love there.

I am in a ball, sobbing uncontrollably, when he touches me. "Aurora."

I startle and cry out, quailing back against the door. "*Don't fucking touch me!*"

"Aurora. I . . . I won't hurt you." His voice, suddenly, is far away. The pain in it unmistakable. "It's not what you think . . ."

"How could you do that?" I sob, pulsing with rage, and choke on the words. My eyes fill with tears. "I was falling for you. I was *falling* for you . . ."

There is a long silence. I cannot tell where he is in that void, but when he speaks again his voice trembles. "Please. Just let me explain."

"Who are you? *What* are you?" I spit. "Were you . . ." My stomach heaves at the words. "Were you *eating her* . . ."

"No. No, I was not."

"Don't lie to me!"

"I would not lie to you, Aurora. I would never do that." There is a long silence, and then, "You want to know what I am?"

I wait, not trusting myself to speak.

"You want to know why I'm so pale?"

No. No.

"Why I shun daylight?"

Please stop.

"Why I drink . . .?"

I turn cold all over. That can't be. That's ridiculous. "You can't . . . There are no . . ." I swallow. "You're just a madman who thinks he is a . . ."

"I can prove it to you, if you wish," he says quietly.

I can't speak for the lump in my throat, and he takes that as my answer.

"There is a porthole. There, on the wall to your left." He pauses. "Open it."

I hesitate, listening. I can't hear any movement at all in that room. Any breathing at all, besides my own terrified pants.

I stand and keep to the wall, away from where I last heard that voice. My hands find a new wall and there, above my head, the cool collar of a baseplate. It's circular, and I can feel a hinge, and two dogs—the fasteners for a storm cover. A deadlight, in maritime parlance.

Every cell in my body is screaming for me to not turn my back on that room, but I do. I unscrew the dogs until those threading devices can be tugged out of their grooves and hinged away.

I hesitate, looking over my shoulder into the blackness.

"Go on," urges Adrian's voice gently.

So I creak the storm cover wide in a protest of rusty hinges.

Glowy daylight flares into a small, unadorned space that's not much bigger than its narrow bed, with a toilet beside it, a bulkhead with rows of dark communication consoles locked behind a thumbprint sensor. Some sort of panic room.

Yeah, sounds about right.

I swallow, palms slick with sweat, and open the storm cover all the way. It judders, its eerie creaking rising, rising, filling the whole room, and my heart is thumping in my throat by the time the round portlight widens like a reverse eclipse and falls on the pale, familiar face of Adrian Voper standing in the middle of the room.

It is only a moment—one infinite, vibrating moment—that our eyes are locked, before his skin begins to smoke.

It hisses and sizzles and black burns bloom like a mold across his face, but he endures it—waiting for my belief to set in, for the hiccups of grief to catch in my throat, and a fume of gray smoke starts up from his head by the time I let out a wracking sob and slam the storm cover shut and yank the dogs back in place.

Nothing to hear in that room, for the longest time, but his anguished breathing. If breathing it is.

And then, at last, "You believe now, I presume?" It comes out hoarse and dry as ash. "You believe that I'm a—"

But I cannot hear him. I cannot hear him for the drumming in my ears, the stench of burnt flesh in my nostrils. How unforgiveable. That even now he can make me pity him.

"Are there others like you?" I whisper at last. "Those guests . . ."

He is silent a long time in that darkness. And then, "Yes."

The bodies in Voper's bed. No normal orgy at all.

"So, what, you're all yacht owners, then?" I snort. A joke.

But he confirms it. A whole new world before me, conjured to shimmering life. "It's easier that way."

"You mean to go where you please, dine as you please?"

". . . Yes." A fatalistic bitterness in his voice.

"How convenient for you," I hiss. "Floating homes, and no one to catch you in international waters. You simply enjoy yourself in one port and move on to the next, is that it?"

Thea's corpse, dropping to the deck. Thea's corpse, dropped over the side.

"Let me explain—"

But I've sucked in a decisive breath. "Get out," I say quietly, and feel him cock his head. "You beast. You *monster*. Get the fuck out!"

"Aurora," he swallows, voice thick with torment. "Please—"

"Get out!" I snarl, teeth gritted, and face that voice with hands fisted. "Get out! *Get out! GET OUT!*"

I'm still screaming by the time the door opens and shuts again.

TWENTY-THREE

It's not long before sleep claims me once more, slumped on the floor against the wall. I dream of hot blood, and darkness, and Adrian Voper standing wan as a corpse in the merciless glare of the rising sun. He lifts a hand toward me, mouth opening in woeful intonation—*Aurora*—and his face bursts into flame.

When I jerk awake the porthole has been opened again, and a beam of late afternoon light slants through the darkness onto Mrs. Colding perched prim and erect on the edge of a chair. I stiffen, and for a moment it flares up in me, the dazzling possibility: escape. She is here for my escape.

But no. That is not why she is here. That is not what she is offering.

She gestures to a chair opposite her. "Please. Have a seat."

Ah.

I grit my teeth, momentarily dizzy with a hard, small murderous anger, and drag myself up. I'm stiff and sore, every muscle in my body crying out as if I've been dropped off a building. For now, I drop into the chair, hoping the puffiness of my eyes isn't visible.

Mrs. Colding considers me a long while before she clears her throat and begins. "Given what's happened, I thought we should—"

"So, then," I interrupt acidly, "that's what you're always up to in his cabin."

Mrs. Colding tilts her head in a question.

"Cleaning up all the blood."

A muscle jumps underneath her eye, but she does not look away.

"What else do you do for him? Help dispose of the bodies?"

This is what she has become in my mind. An old woman with a cunning smile, a sly servant of vice.

But Mrs. Colding folds her hands neatly in her lap and sighs, as if she cannot be bothered to be offended. "Anger is to be expected, but let's dispense with the sarcasm, shall we?"

Even here, even now, my cheeks can flush, I can feel the sting of embarrassment. But I am not to be so easily fended off. "How often does this happen?" I push on, holding her eyes.

She blinks, swallows. A tiny crack in her composure. "More often, lately."

I think back on red blood on white snow, red stains on white sheets, and gooseflesh prickles my arms. "So Emmie wasn't a hallucination, then," I whisper, frigid with fury. "You *gaslighted* me—"

"Aurora . . ."

"You let me think I was going *insane*—"

"I . . . feel remorse about that. I had to protect my employer."

"Your employer," I scoff, and shake my head. When I speak again, my voice is more controlled. "Who else knows?"

"Just the captain and I." She is smooth and to the point, on firmer ground now. We are having a perfectly normal conversation. "Jason has his suspicions."

Oh, I bet he does. I think of his attempt to warn me at my cabin door, and draw in a measured breath. "How long have you worked for him?"

Her mouth twitches faintly. "A long time."

I can summon it now: the full force of my disgust. "How?" I breathe. "How can you?"

She does not rise to this. Instead, a pitying contempt enters her eyes. As if to say, *How can this little girl possibly know? How can she know how mysterious this world is, with its humbling, harrowing events that shape us into much larger versions of ourselves, full of a terrible capacity for acceptance and compromise?*

But in the end, all she says—all she has to say—is this: "I know what it's like to lose someone, and be forced into becoming a stranger to yourself."

I blink as if struck. "Lose . . .?"

She arches a brow, a delicate movement. "Did he not tell you about his wife?"

My gut tumbles. *His wife?*

Her eyes glint, she sighs. "Like all of us, he has his reasons for why he is the way he is."

My throat is suddenly dry. "What—what was she like?"

I am regarded with a cool distance, as if I have asked a question we both know I will not like the answer to. "Very beautiful," is the pithy reply. "Her name was Evangeline. She was fiery, strict, obsessed with order. Musicians usually are."

Insides still twisting pathetically with jealousy, I think of Adrian's mournful piano playing haunting the *Lair*. "She was a pianist?"

Mrs. Colding nods. "A sensation, by all accounts. When she'd perform, the stage would be buried in roses."

Roses.

"What happened to her?"

Mrs. Colding hesitates, brushes at her skirt. "They were to begin a new life together," she says finally. Her voice is light, carefully detached. "They were madly in love. He wanted to support her in touring her music, and she wanted to give him a family, as he'd always wished to be a family man. They had never been happier in their lives. And so it was that they set sail on a ship on their wedding night, and in the dark hours, as they were strolling the deck, something white as chalk dropped down on them out of the shrouds . . ."

My blood runs cold.

Mrs. Colding shifts in her chair, clears her throat. "It was . . . one of *them*. You may have heard him mentioned last night—the Commodore." Her throat bobs again.

"Volok is his name." I feel a shiver, as if a cold wind had blown into the room, and Mrs. Colding shivers herself at the invocation of the name. She glances about, as if, absurdly, someone may have heard, and continues. "He is the oldest of them. And the most feared. And that night, he was hungry . . ."

No.

"That silent drop from above knocked Voper unconscious. When he came to, Volok was feeding on her. He was feeding on his wife. Her eyes open and staring at him, unblinking, as her life pooled out on the deck . . ."

I shut my eyes, hearing it. The howl of despair.

Mrs. Colding draws herself back from a faraway place. "It was the ending of his world. He tried to save her, but the thing turned and gave him a cold embrace. The worst thing this Volok could have done. To make Voper live forever in his grief." She drops her eyes, and when she speaks again, her voice has thickened. "He never got over it. And in his mourning—his *feeding*—it's as if he has . . ."

And it clicks in place, the final, horrific piece of the puzzle: "She was *blonde*."

A slow nod. "Yes."

"They're all blondes."

Mrs. Colding sighs, a reluctant schoolmistress. "Lust and bloodlust—they are two sides of the same coin for them. One brings on the other. And so, for Voper, it's as if with every blonde beauty he gorges on, he is trying to recapture—"

"Stop," I hiss, shutting my eyes. "Just stop."

The thoughts rage through me, black and maddening and clotted with fear. Lucia. Emmie. Thea.

But not me.

I shake my head. It doesn't make any sense. "But I'm not . . ." I begin. "Why . . ."

"Because you're not like the rest," Mrs. Colding whispers, leaning forward in her urgency. "He has been stuck this way for so long, trapped in his perfect little world, he has forgotten who he is. But you . . . You have cracked the ice, Arie. You have woken something in him, and he doesn't know what to do anymore."

Doesn't know what to do.

Voper, pulling away when he first kissed me. Pulling away when we made love, so he would not give in to instinct and destroy me.

Destroying Thea instead.

I gasp in air, feeling my gorge rise. I blink away tears. "I think . . ."

"Arie." Mrs. Colding's face falls. "It's not your fault . . ."

But I'm standing from my chair and backing away, tears spilling down my cheeks. "I think I need time. I need time to think."

Mrs. Colding rises, an aching sadness in her face. "Of course. I'll leave you alone." She opens the door—it was unlocked all along—and leaves it open. She gestures, and I dimly recognize the adjoining space beyond: Voper's master suite. "It's yours, if you promise to be good. We can't let you out into the yacht for now, as I'm sure you can understand. But I hope—I very much hope—that we'll get there." She straightens, dispassionate professionalism returned, and confers me a look of somber encouragement. "I'll see you soon, Miss Strand."

When she goes, I shut my eyes and sway back and forth in that room.

This is how. This is how you can be caught between two worlds and not know how you got there.

TWENTY-FOUR

I emerge on tenterhooks into the lair of the *Lair*.

It's close to what I remember: a windowless womb with monolithic canvases of red paint on the walls, vases of red roses on the nightstands. The bed with its crimson coverlet, however, is neatly made. No mussed sheets, no writhing bodies. No things of the night preying on female flesh.

On the bed my bags of clothing, a tray steaming with dinner. How civilized.

They did not give me my cell phone, though.

My curiosity overcomes my fear—I have to inspect the full suite. But there is nothing to be gleaned about its owner. The dressing room is a maze of shiny wood screens, racks of bespoke suits, drawers of silk ties and brushed leather shoes and luxury watches floating like strange baubles in cubic watch winders—the usual accoutrements of a mystery man. The bathroom barren, sterile, no condiments to be seen. A shaving kit for an undead body? Not required.

The one conspicuous detail: a pair of heavy crimson drapes opposite the bed.

There can't be, I know, a window behind those drapes, as it doesn't face the sea. Perhaps that is why my hands are shaking when I reach out and yank them wide.

But no locker full of bodies greets my eyes. It's merely a painting—a rather large painting. Perhaps four feet tall by three feet wide. Its frame is ornately carved, and very old, for it's been scratched and chipped, here and there, with blonde wood showing through, like lighted bone. And dominating the canvas: a woman, very beautiful in an intense, classical way, in a high-collared dress.

It is because of the eyes, the dark blue eyes blazing back at me with passionate, haughty arrogance, that I only gradually register that her hair is blonde.

Blonde. A woman with blonde hair. A blonde-haired woman.

His wife.

I snap the curtains shut and lie back, trembling, on the bed.

It is soft, deep, luxurious, and I think—desperate to forget the loveliness of Evangeline Voper—of how many times it has borne his weight. How many years. How old is he?

A ship, she said. A sailing ship. What would that make it, then? A hundred years? Two hundred?

What, truly, would a woman mean to him? What would he want in a woman, when he has seen so much, experienced so much?

The usual things, no doubt.

But no. There is nothing usual about this. About him.

Hot, debilitating shame flares my cheeks. What is wrong with me? Why do I care? *He's a fucking vampire, Aurora.*

I close my eyes, breathing in the faint scent of roses, and will my thoughts elsewhere. So this is his life. This pleasure boat gliding along the Côte d'Azur like a specter of death, leaving blood-churned waters in its wake. The drained corpses of supermodels hung in closets or tossed overboard. I think of his life in the offseason, long winter nights wandering the empty yacht alone—his orderly solitude, his systematic reading, his mournful piano playing echoing through the cabins and passageways.

Emptiness. Grief. Rage. Bloodlust.

Forever.

What kind of fool would I be, to not run from that? And what kind of heartless fraud, to leave him to it?

For this is what it comes down to. The fear that to be with him would be a defeat, some kind of capitulation. What would Cailee think of me? What would I think of myself? For there would be compromises, certainly, and uncomfortable accommodations, as in any partnership. His would merely be a more particular and trying kind.

Would he want me to watch? Would he want me to join him? Is that what it would mean, to be with him?

What horror, what quaking shame.

How would I live with myself? To be party to that—mistress to a monster. How could I look myself in the eye?

How could I sleep in this bed in which so many women had died?

I jump off it, skin crawling, and end up huddled against the wall with my knees hugged to my chest. Who am I fooling? This won't last. Not after Josh. How could I subject myself to that again? How could I be with another abuser? What would that do to my trauma?

All the same, the thought is there: Would it not be a kind of sin to refuse this offer? Out of a notion of morality, or fearfulness. For does he not need saving? I have woken something in him, she said. And was there not pain in his voice earlier? A harrowed self-hatred?

Not to say anything of the fact—the trembling, incandescent fact—of my desire for him.

All around me, the feeling—that I'm cornered, that I'm in danger of giving up, or may already have.

But would it be giving up, to give in?

Would it?

TWENTY-FIVE

The days pass. In that sunless suite, the only way to track them is by the serving of my meals. Mrs. Colding, three times a day, bustling through the door with a tray. The shamefaced indignity of watching her service the room. And then the silence afterwards, the crushing loneliness.

She never comments on the sheets I've dragged onto the floor. She understands why I wouldn't sleep in that bed.

Yoga only does so much for my aching muscles, and forget about distracting me from my thoughts. I think of escape, but my fingerprint on the communication console sensor is denied. Big surprise.

Next, I think of Adrian. I've gone through it countless times, and still I return to the same question: If I stayed, would I leave if it got bad enough? Or am I the kind of woman who wants to be treated this way?

I pace the suite, restless, anger rising. The unfairness, the sheer craziness of it all, begins to sink in. I bang on the door and scream until my throat is raw. I throw things. I curse and plead. I weep.

The next time Mrs. Colding comes through the door with a tray, she finds me curled up in Adrian's bed, exhausted and half-asleep. When I open my eyes and see her there, she's smiling.

As the days trudge on and the *Lair* knifes through God knows what waters, I slip into a trancelike calm.

I sleep in Adrian's bed and wonder if I dream his dreams.

I soak in his bath, remembering the way his skin felt on mine.

I watch the slice of light under the door, wondering if his shadow will darken it.

It's on the ninth night that it does.

I suffer waves of trembling, for I know: It can't be Mrs. Colding. The lock turns, the door opens, and there is the outline I could pick out in a crowd, framed by the dim light of the hallway beyond.

Do not come in, I think. *I am not ready. I still have no idea of what to think of you. Of us.*

But he does come. At least, his voice does—it is low, halting, and full of courtesy. "Hello, Aurora."

I should hate him, I know. I should hate him in this moment.

And still, what his voice can do to me. The goose bumps it raises, for all the chill that touches my throat.

"Hello, Adrian," I whisper back.

He glides forward, and I instinctively stiffen and retreat.

He rocks to a halt, his hands fisting at his sides, and turns his face away. It is too dark to see him, to see if his face is still charred and blackened by the sun. And the thought comes to me: Ten feet or less. Ten feet between me and the thing of teeth and bloodlust in the shadows.

At last, he lifts his face. "I know you have every reason to not trust me right now. Every reason to loathe me." His hands tremble, his body wired tight with a haggard woundedness. "I know that. But I . . ." His voice falters, suddenly young and pure and blistering with hope. "But I would very much like to show you something. If you'd let me."

Adrian Voper—always full of surprises.

This is where I spit in his face. This is where I tell him to go to hell.

But I'm walking. Step by step I walk up to him, my breath shivering out between my lips, until I'm within reach of those hands.

Our eyes meet, and he smiles.

His hand goes into his pocket and comes out with a slip of black cloth. He lifts it toward my eyes, and I tense—a blindfold.

But his eyes hold mine. He makes a shushing noise, as if I were a wild foal. "It's okay," he says. "It's okay."

How foolish, I think. How foolish would I have to be to submit to this? To trust a vampire about to blindfold me?

Very, is the answer. For I do, God help me. Maybe I've been locked up for too long, or something's wrong with me, but I let him. He drops the blindfold before my eyes, twists and snugs it tight behind my head, and all is a scratchy black, the blood booming in my ears. And then the touch of his hand in mine, like an offering.

Our fingers curve around each other, and he leads me through darkness—through his world.

On and on, down twisting hallways through the boat. At some point he must come to a staircase, for suddenly he has swept his arm under my legs—my heart leaps into my throat—and he is carrying me, my face against his chest. Memories rush back to me, and I breathe in his scent, curling my fingers against his shirt. Maybe all is well. All is right here. Whatever is to come, I can accept it.

And then I am down again. He is guiding my feet into tall fuzzy boots, my arms into sleeves, slipping something puffy and warm onto me. Then a zipper seals me in, a lock clicks back. "You'll feel cold," he says, and I do—a blast of frigid air. The breath sears in my lungs. My ears are instantly frostbitten.

"Holy *shit*," I manage, teeth chattering. "Where the hell *are* we?"

But then his hands are in my hair, the blindfold falls away. I hear his smile in my ear. "Take a guess."

And I look up and see the light.

It's everywhere. Hanging in brilliant, shimmering veils of radiance across the night sky, blurred into phantasmic curtains in all colors, as if another world had spilled into this one—a fantastic mirage, a miracle of light. It's so sudden, so overwhelming in its uncanny green glow whorling off into gentler, more gauzy shades, that it's hard to believe there are actually colors like this in existence, lights like this.

The Northern Lights.

The full recognition of his gift hits me. Tears spring to my eyes. My knees go watery. I turn to him, and there he is—mostly recovered from his sacrificial tan, though here and there his skin is still pulled tight or shines raw and pink as a newborn's beneath the dry, dead patches that are flaking away. But I don't see that. Because he's smiling at me with such dazzling happiness that I feel dizzy for a moment, and all my worries are swept away as if a dam has broken.

"How . . ." I splutter. "Where . . ."

"We're in Norway," he explains. "Somewhere off Tromvik. I had the captain get us here in record time." I turn to see the *Lair* floats on ice-cold waters mirroring the eerie green light show in the sky, and beyond this bay snow-capped mountains gleam with a clean white fire. They're as dazzling as his smile.

When I look into his eyes again, he's studying me with a look of such pure devotion it makes everything inside me melt. "So, Aurora," he says, grinning. "What do you think of your namesake?"

"I—I don't—" I flounder, gesturing. The words don't come. There are no words for what I'm feeling. He smiles, tiny dimples bracketing the edges of his mouth, and pulls up the fur-fringed hood of my parka—I've been shivering, and didn't even notice. I must look like a muskrat with pneumonia.

"I was hoping they'd be here," he says. "They're rare in late summer." His hands linger on the hood, one thumb brushing my cheek. I spark at his touch.

Then he cranes his head up at the ever-changing veils of light, dark eyes full of uncanny green swirls, and a wistful look passes over his face. "It is beautiful, isn't it?" he says, and when he says it, I know. I know he means more than just these lights above us. "I'd forgotten how beautiful it could be . . ." His lips lift just the slightest bit, showing a hint of sharpness, and it comes back to me—the cruel reality that has been nudging at the edge of my thoughts, ready to spring. And I think, *Not yet. Let me stay here, in this moment.*

He must sense this, for when he turns to me again his face is more melancholic than I've ever seen it. "I want you to know," he begins, and clears his throat. "That what you saw that night . . . that wasn't me. The person who gave you this . . . *that's* what I am. Or what I want to be." He gropes for the words, but they slip through his fingers to the deck. "And ever since I met you . . ."

I nod, I can do that for him. I reach up and touch his cheek. "I know."

He quickly holds my hand there and shuts his eyes, and I have to swallow a sudden swelling of emotion in my throat.

"Please," he says. "Please don't leave me."

"I won't," I promise, a sob rising in me, and dash a tear from my eye. "I won't."

And he holds my hand to his cheek as the world turns and the aurora coruscates overhead like a vampire's dream of the sun.

TWENTY-SIX

We are shy and chaste with one another as he escorts me back inside the *Lair*, like teenagers grown bashful after a first kiss. And then the bubbling up of anxiety as we near his suite. What is expected here? Will he hope to—

But I put a stop to this line of worry. I turn before the red double doors and look up into his face. "I'm not ready yet."

He nods, a grave and gentle amusement there. "I know."

"I just need time."

"I'll wait." And he does, knowing I need to say more.

At last, I pluck up the courage. "If this is to work—if we're going to do this—I need to feel safe."

"And what can I do to make you feel that?"

"I need to feel you trust me. With . . . what you are."

"Ah." His eyes dance. "I thought you'd say that." And before I can say a word, he takes my hand and lifts it to his lips, the touch raising the fine hairs on my arm. His lips crimp in a smile, and when I turn my hand over, there—as if by magic—is my cell phone returned to me.

My breath stops, I look up with furrowed brows—but he's gone.

My thoughts linger on him as I shut the double doors and lock them, slip into the cool sheets of his bed. Where is he now? Does he have another lair inside the *Lair*? Does he even sleep? I think of him standing before the glass expanse of the underwater observation lounge, hands in pockets, waiting for the sun to come up—and for when he'll see me again.

I turn my phone over in my hands, and when I touch the home button and the screen lights up with Cailee's flurry of worried texts, I feel the full weight of Adrian's gesture. The power he's given me.

Reveal what I am, if you wish. Reveal my secrets.

Another touch of the button, and my thumb hovers over the lock screen. Trembles.

I shove the phone away and shut my eyes.

I wake to a knock on the double doors. For one breathless, infinite moment I think it will be him. But no. It is Mrs. Colding waiting there in the hallway, hands crossed and not batting an eye. "Good morning, Miss Strand," she sniffs. "Breakfast will be on the aft bridge deck when you're ready." The corner of her mouth twitches, as if in obscure approval of something, and she sweeps away down the hall.

So. She is glad, then. She is glad I've chosen to stay.

As I shut the door, I can't help but wonder when I'll see him again. Sundown? Sooner? And the urge comes—as if in reaction to the nature of what he is—to feel alive, to feel the sun on my skin.

After a solitary breakfast I change into a frilly black bikini with cheeky bottoms and head for the sun lounge at the bow of the *Lair*. As I pass the bridge a side door slides open and Captain Redfearn pulls up short when he sees me. He opens his mouth to speak, then tips his hat. "Miss Strand," he intones in a cautious sea-dog growl, and slips past as if terrified of breaking me.

He knows, then. He knows I'm seeing Adrian.

A far different reaction from the gaggle of deckhands polishing the anchor housing. They gape as I practice my catwalk sass to the sun lounge. Whispers fly—"I thought he got rid of her?", "Where did *she* come from?"—and Jason pales mid-bark, looking sick to his stomach at the sight of me. I smirk and lift my chin—"As you were, boys"—and strut on, ass cheeks jiggling, exulting in my own skin. I don't know what's gotten into me. I feel renewed, transformed, giddy with nerves.

I feel *hot*.

But no, it's not just a feeling. It's realizing at long last: I *am* hot.

Perhaps it's the glow of being singled out, so unexpectedly chosen. Perhaps it's the knowledge that *I'm* the model on the boat now. My turn to shine.

Or perhaps it's simply that making a choice for myself has finally given me a taste of what real power feels like.

The power of knowing I could turn Adrian in at any moment.

Jason is powerless against it. He drifts toward me with a determined look, his question like an opening salvo. "So you're back."

I arch a brow at him. "What makes you think I ever left?"

His face slackens in disbelief. "You chose to stay?"

"Haven't you?" I sass right back.

He scowls and shifts his weight, taken aback. "I just—" He crosses his burly arms, the dragon on his bicep coiling angrily. "I didn't think you would."

A small, complex indignance stirs in me. "Oh? And why's that?"

But he presses his lips together.

I let out a breath through my nose with a derisive "I see." And then, "It's different because I'm a girl, huh? But you get a free pass?"

He only simmers, and I wonder how long he's been stewing on this. Or had he thought I'd gone the way of Adrian's previous playthings? Perhaps he'd been torn up about it, his relief was now mixed up with his jealousy and this was how it was coming out.

But I don't have the patience to sort this out. I cock a hip. "Did you have anything else to say?" I lift a bottle of suntan lotion. "Or were you just hoping I'd let you lather me up?"

His eyes flash. He takes a step forward, finger lifted—and freezes, glancing over his shoulder.

Something happens in his face and he gives me one last conflicted look before turning away, teeth gritted. What stopped him?

That's when I feel Adrian's eyes on me.

I lift my gaze to check, and it's true. A lone shadow in a suit stands at the darkly tinted windows lining the forward observation deck. There's something odd, even unsettling, about his face. As if he were wearing a gas mask. And it comes to me: binoculars. His face is half-hidden by the binoculars he is looking through. Looking through to watch me.

I am trembling when I lie down on the warm sun pad and watch the bow glide smoothly over the waves.

My mind turns expansive, reflective. I force my hands to lie still on the pad on either side of me. I have a hard time controlling my breathing. My taut tummy trembles, sucking in and out, swelling my ribcage. This is how it must be. These are the factors that give tension to this game. Him, trapped inside by the sun, unable to do anything but watch. Me, out here, torturing him with my body. This is our unspoken agreement.

I am aware Jason is looking on, sick with jealousy, but I do not think of that. He is not a part of this.

I wait, and wonder—idly, distantly—how I will react to Adrian Voper's eyes on me.

I can't help it. I shift and adjust in a self-conscious settling of my flesh, sweat-tacky skin sticking to the pad—the uneasiness of a mate, or prey. I stretch my arms indolent and catlike above me, and my outthrust breasts pillow generously in my bikini top. My knees, drawn up, show off the womanly angle of my thighs. I don't have to look to sense the concentrated intensity of his excitement, and my toes curl into the sun pad. I can feel a glow suffusing me, my body quivering in a series of involuntary twitches. I am flushed with the giddiness of offering myself up to this assault—of implying an invitation. I am mesmerized, blasted with amazement. It is unbearable.

So. This is what he can do. This is the effect he can still have on me.

This is the place he still has in my world.

TWENTY-SEVEN

I see him again at dinner. When Mrs. Colding leads me into the dining room with its glittering chandelier hanging through the ceiling above, he is waiting at the end of the long table, resplendent in a beautiful dark brown suit, black dress shirt and no tie. Something registers—that he hasn't worn a tie for weeks now, that the color of his suit is the warmest I've seen him in yet—but I don't know what it means.

Also, I note with a distracting fluttering of my stomach, there's no trace of his encounter with the sun now. His face is as fresh and pure as snow.

He rises when I enter, blue eyes large and avid. "You freckle when you get sun."

I feel my cheeks grow warm. "I thought you hated freckles."

"Yes." His face takes on a pensive cast. "I thought I did, too."

We stare at each other a moment before I tear my eyes away. I could drown in those liquid blue pools.

That's when I notice that Captain Redfearn and Mrs. Colding are watching me from the shadows at the far end of the room, like parents witnessing a bride being presented to a barbarous groom.

My knees are shaking as I sit.

Adrian follows suit, tugging at his cuffs. There's a vase of splendid red roses in the center of the table. My gaze must linger on it, for Adrian purses his lips, gestures and Mrs. Colding whisks it away and ascends a staircase in her soft-soled shoes. Captain Redfearn is nowhere to be seen.

It's very quiet when Adrian speaks again. "Not a fan of roses?"

I shrug. "I'm a white lily gal myself."

How aware, how very aware I am, that I am alone with him.

I straighten my back, perched on the edge of my seat, and link my fingers on the table. "I have questions."

He smirks, faintly amused, and mirrors me, linking his long, pale fingers on the table: business meeting accepted. "Of course."

"How old are you?"

"A hundred and seventy-two years old. I was thirty-three when I was turned."

Jesus Christ. "How many of you are there?"

"Not many. A few hundred. Perhaps a thousand. We took to the sea a long time ago. It's not safe for us on land. Too easily cornered, found out. So we made investments, accumulated wealth over the years"—he gestures at the grandness about us—"and made ourselves new homes."

I wet my lips. "How does it work? Like, are there rules—"

"We have our laws." A small, tight smile appears on his perfect lips. "There are repercussions, for instance, for those who draw attention to us."

"Are there, I don't know, other kinds of creatures out there?"

His eyes crinkle in that way of theirs. "Not that I'm aware of."

It's hard to look him in the eye. The question hovers on my lips, the question this entire conversation has been driving toward.

At last, I ask it: "Do you want to feed on me?"

That pale white face slackens. When he speaks, his voice is low, husky, trembling with yearning. "Yes."

I swallow, the edges of my vision blurring, and something becomes dislodged in me, that memory of Josh I thought I'd put away forever, consigned to darkness and oblivion. *Oh no*, I think, *not now*, and shut my eyes. "Are you going to?"

"No." The word is bare, scraped raw. "You're the first woman since I've been turned who has made me want to resist that."

My hands are trembling; I slide them into my lap. I feel as if I am coming undone. I can see him. Josh. Ordering me to tell Cailee to go home, his face ugly, a stranger's. He didn't like seeing me happy around other people. He wanted to fuck. To prove I loved him.

"That's good," I stammer, my mouth dry. "Because . . ."

Because I told him no that night. I'd never refused him before.

He did not like that.

"Yes?" Adrian says in the dining room of the *Lair*, his brow furrowed.

I force my voice steady, sweat gathering on the backs of my legs, making them stick to my chair. I'm trembling all over now. I feel as if I'm going to be sick. "Because I was with a man who was . . . who was . . ."

And there it is, my evil talisman—what I thought I'd forgotten. The memory of Josh at his sinister work. The look on his face when I woke later that night, and found him pulling my shorts to my knees . . .

My dark secret. The thing I hate about myself. The thing I thought I'd left behind in Oregon, come back to me.

Always trying to define me.

"And I can't," I half-gasp at last, having to remember how to speak, how to be a person again, the hot tears building behind my eyelids. "I can't do that again."

Adrian studies me with his blue-black eyes. He knows something momentous has just been shared, but does not know what. He looks as if he wants to rise out of his chair, perhaps to comfort me. But he forces himself still. "I can't change what I am," he says finally in a careful, haunted voice. "But I promise: I will never do anything to you that you don't want me to."

Something small and humbling flutters inside me. "So, you wish you weren't"—I wave a hand—"what you are?"

His eyes drop in a grimace. "Yes."

"Why?" I ask, hearing the test in my voice. I gesture at the wealth around us. "Why give all this up? Isn't this life what everyone wants?"

He lets out a wry snort. "Is it? My feeding . . . it's a *need*. I will not deny there is a . . . *hideous ecstasy*." He studies his open hands, a murderer's hands, his eyes glittering. "But that does not mean I love my violence. Or am ignorant to the fact that it does not bring me love."

So he knows that, at least.

He closes his hands, a stoniness in his voice now. "This is not what I want. I have never wanted this." The veins in his knuckles bulge. "I have tried to kill myself. Many times."

Many times.

He's never told anyone this. I can tell by the angry clenching of his jaw, the skittering of his eyes. And so I ask my next question, to rescue him from the terrible silence that's fallen between us. "Can you be turned back?"

He thinks on it, his brow creasing. "Yes, if the vampire who turned me was killed. But Volok . . ." He shakes his head. An impossible notion. When he looks up, his eyes burn. "But I have you now. If you'll have me."

I suck in a long, measured breath. "What do you expect here? Do you want me to—"

"No. No, I would never ask that of you."

"Good. Because I'd never become like you."

He winces, nods. That had been expected.

The next question hovers in the back of my throat, waiting to be asked: *When will he feed again? And how will I feel when he does?*

But I push this away. I'm not ready to think about that.

"So, if we were to . . . I'd just grow old, and you'd never change . . ."

"Yes."

I think on that. Would it be bearable? To fall prey to the harrowing indignities of age, while he remained perfect, unchanged and glistening with youth?

At least he'd been honest with me. There was that to hold to as we glided on—through these uncharted, perilous waters—into the next stage of our lives.

He hated his violence, after all. He was not Josh. I was not breaking my promise to myself. My promise to never let another man do violence against me.

I lift my eyes. "Okay, then."

"You gotta be *kidding* me," Cailee growls through the phone. "You actually did it. You seduced a yacht owner. And you haven't called me in weeks because, what? You've been locked up in his suite as his plaything?"

I bite my lip, cringing inside. "Something like that."

"My God. Where are you now?"

"Back to the Med, I think?"

"*Back?*"

"Well, he took me to see the Northern Lights . . ."

Uproarious laughter. "Okay, okay. I'm starting to like him."

I can't help but grin as I pace Adrian's suite. Again, he'd said good night at the door, like some gentleman caller in an old story, knowing he shouldn't push it. And again, I can't get my thoughts off him.

Cailee finally gets her laughter under control. "Sooo, did he confess his dark secret to you?"

My throat goes dry. "Um, yeah. He did."

"And?"

"He, uh . . ." I put a hand to my brow. What to tell her? "It's complicated."

But somehow she senses it anyway. "He's violent, isn't he?"

A long, brittle silence. Cailee sighs. "Babe . . ."

"Okay, he is, but . . . not the way you think."

"So he's just another Josh, then." Her voice has gone flat. "What are you doing?"

"You wouldn't understand."

"Oh, is that right?" she flares in that tone of hers that means she has a hand on her hip.

After a moment, she softens. "Has he hurt you?"

"*No*," I snap, feeling small and cornered. "And he won't."

"What, you're gonna change him?"

I stop. "What?"

"Arie, you can't change him."

Change him. The idea unfurls in my brain like a storm, outrageous and unbidden, and I sink onto the edge of the bed as I think of how people do that, in ordinary relationships with all of their extraordinary mysteries. And how one would do that with Adrian Voper.

TWENTY-EIGHT

There's a lot to consider.

As we head back to the warm waters of the Med, Adrian's many particularities become apparent. His clothing can only be washed in the best mineral water. He likes to read printed news, not digital, so it's a common sight to see the stewardesses ironing newspapers in the morning. He also likes blueberries when he first gets up, so each one has to be dipped in mineral water and buffed with silk until it shines.

No direct criticism for me, but subtle corrections. *This* silverware must be used before *that* silverware.

One day he plucks a blueberry from a fruit bowl, and promptly fires the stewardess on the spot.

There are times when I am so happy after our encounters—dazzled and safe—that I find it hard to breathe. Other times I lie in bed like a stone, eyes welling because of a perceived disappointment, or some offhand comment that had cut me to the core.

You don't have to chew so loudly.

One time, I try. I try to get the words out. "Why do you have to—"

"What?" He looks at me, blue eyes piercing.

But I can't. The sudden, diminishing attention brings on a familiar sweat of anxiety.

"Never mind."

I go to the rail on the main deck as I mull this over, the midday sun beating on my face. Was it fair for him to have said that? To say things like that. But then I think of where this is coming from. The roses. The piano playing. The stuffy, exacting standards of presentation. It was all him honoring her, wasn't it? His wife. Honoring their old life together. Was that so wrong?

Or am I making excuses again? Should I be putting up with this when I'm the one in his life now?

As Cailee would say, *Dafuq is this nonsense?*

I have to remind myself, though: It's not personal. This is Adrian here; it's nothing new. He treats everyone this way, doesn't he? What pampered and psychologically damaged billionaire wouldn't?

The voice at my shoulder agrees. "I know how you feel."

It's the captain. Captain Redfearn has joined me, thumbs hooked into his belt as he squints out at the sparkling water. I'd almost forgotten he's on the boat.

"Yeah?"

He nods. "You get used to it. Sort of."

"Sort of." We sneak a glance at each other, cracking sly grins. *Uh-huh.*

After a while, he sobers. His voice distant with thought. "We don't choose how we deal with our grief. But we can choose how we let it go."

The statement is like a wire zinging through my whole body. I glance at him. I hadn't seen this. I hadn't seen this side of Arnold Redfearn. I had conveniently tucked him away in my mind as a man who lived in fear of his boss, not as a man who had chosen to stay on as captain of the *Lair* out of his own free will, and who had his own reasons for doing so.

He peers at me, years of mysterious experience wrinkled into the skin about his gray eyes. "I hope you help him find a way, Miss Strand."

And he wanders off, back to the bridge deck and his duties.

I hope you help him find a way.

I have that to think of as I walk the boat's main deck, admiring its sparkling perfection and knowing Jason must have been up hours ago to have it washed down in time before the guests (which would now include me) got up. What had the first mate glimpsed, over the years, in those dark hours before the sun's rising? What nocturnal happenings had led him to suspect Adrian's nature?

A sudden moment of déjà vu as I stop to stare. The panels. The panels of the pool roof are open. But this time, during the day.

I step to the edge and peer down.

Floating in the pool—luxuriously floating and basking in the sun that never invades that space—is Jason.

He's only in swimming trunks, golden and glistening, his abs like smooth stones under his radiant skin. My God, he is cut.

A sickening disgust wells up in me, which is quickly replaced by the anger blaring in my skull like alarm bells.

"Hey!"

Jason opens his eyes, almost lazily.

"You can't be in there! That's Adrian's spot—"

"Not during the day, it is," he drawls and shuts his eyes, tipping his head back again.

Steam comes out of my ears. Does he know? Is he making a joke?

I don't really care.

I'm down there in the space of a minute, stopping at the edge to glare at him with hands on hips. "What do you think you're doing?"

His lips curl up in a dreamy smile. "So protective, for a woman who's with a man who has everything."

That stings. What's wrong with me? Why am I acting like Adrian right now? Jesus, is he rubbing off on me?

But I shake this off. Fuck that. I'm not the one acting like an overgrown child here.

"Is this a regular thing for you, then?"

Jason considers me behind the crack in his eyelids, seemingly enjoying this. He's different today, full of an affected languor and detachment; it makes me want to scream. How is he not terrified of being caught? Doesn't he know he'd be not only fired on the spot, but blackballed from the yachting industry forever? What has gotten into him?

"Well? Aren't you on shift right now?" I snap.

He hauls himself dripping out of the water, sits on the edge and slicks his hair back. "Voper and Mrs. Colding are having a meeting." He shrugs his massive shoulders. "I have some time." His arms, braced on either side of him, flare with idly flexing engines of muscle, and when he looks up into my eyes with a self-satisfied smirk, it hits me: He's showing off. He's doing exactly what I did to him.

But this is different. He's showing me what I can't have with Adrian: a man, golden and warm-blooded, glowing with life.

A petty, preening anger, intended to provoke.

The little shit.

But he's not little. That is obvious—that is very obvious—when he lies back on his elbows so we both have a better view of each other. A view of the skin that's revealed, and the skin that's not. He lets me soak in his burly Adonis form, achingly chiseled and beaded with water droplets, for a long moment before he says it. "You're looking a little peaky, Miss Strand." The gloating triumph in his voice is so intense I want to smack the smirk off his face, smack myself for being stupid enough to be lured down here. "Is there anything Mr. Billionaire isn't giving you?"

"Nothing at all," I spit and storm away.

TWENTY-NINE

The next morning, I sit in a fog of sulky annoyance at breakfast. It all starts with me ordering a peach Bellini and smoked salmon and crème fraiche omelet and taking a walk about the boat, as Adrian doesn't like to be disturbed during his morning reading of the news. When I return, my omelet is waiting for me in a sprinkling of cheese with hash browns and two charred vine tomatoes on the side, my Bellini a champagne glass of fizzing sunshine. I rub my hands together and press them to my lips, giggling in anticipation.

But Adrian is all frowns as I sit. "You're late."

"What's that?"

"You're late. For the meal."

I stare. "It's *breakfast*."

But as I reach for my silverware roll, he continues. "It's rude to not be present when a meal is served."

I drop my hands into my lap and turn to him, brow raised.

He shrugs, cutting into his morning steak. "Chefs take it as an insult. My chef used to work for Arab royalty, and you're eating his offering while it's cold."

I bite back a retort, feeling the steam gather in my ears. "I'll remember that next time," I simper through a frozen smile, but leave the omelet untouched, thinking of what Captain Redfearn had said. Jason had said.

Mrs. Colding comes by, offering to take it from me, but Adrian holds out a hand. "She's not done."

Mrs. Colding darts a look at me. Retreats. "Of course."

Time crawls by. I'm mesmerized by the blood and juices eddying in Adrian's plate when he lifts his head, scenting the air. "What is that?"

I look up. Mrs. Colding, on her way back to the galley, slows and turns, a remote guardedness entering her eyes. "Pardon?"

Adrian scans the roses festooning the bridge deck, the bouquet on the table. He cups a bud. "They're turning."

Mrs. Colding lifts her brows, darts a look at me. "They were delivered just three days ago—"

"Then why do they look like this?" Adrian sweeps the bouquet out of its vase and brandishes it under her nose. "Hmm?"

I swallow a lump in my throat, place a hand on his arm. "Adrian, it's only—"

But Adrian lifts a hand, eyes never leaving Mrs. Colding. "You know this upsets me. Why would you deliberately upset me?" His teeth are clenched. He flings the roses to the deck and Mrs. Colding flinches, but stands her ground.

"Adrian!" I snap.

"This is most disappointing, Mrs. Colding." Adrian shakes his head, disgusted.

That's quite enough of that, thank you.

The words are out before I can stop myself. "Don't speak to her like that."

The slow, astonished turn of the head from Adrian is all the signal Mrs. Colding needs. She purses her lips and bows, already half-turning away. "I'll take my leave—"

"No." Before I know it my chair has shrilled back and I'm on my feet, the blood surging in my temples. "I want you to hear this."

Mrs. Colding freezes, face tight, and side-eyes Adrian. His eyes have never left me. What is that expression? Does he know what's coming next?

Too bad. He's going to get it anyway.

"You don't know what you've got, do you?" I launch in. "Mrs. Colding lives to serve you and your little world with all its rules. Would anyone else do that? Would anyone else be so loyal to you, knowing what you are? She's been too professional to tell me, but my guess is that she lost a partner of her own, and so she is uniquely suited to understand your pain. And this is how you repay her?"

Adrian rolls his eyes and huffs, "Don't presume to understand—"

"Oh, but I will," I cut him off, and he blinks in surprise. "There's not much to understand, really. Mrs. Colding is impeccable. She can be cold-blooded, and half the time I live in terror of her, but she runs this ship tighter than a facelift. All to your specifications. And despite all that, guess what? You *still* don't appreciate her. You don't appreciate anyone. You are so trapped in this little world you've constructed for yourself that you have forgotten what it's like to be alive. To treat others with respect."

I am vaguely aware that Mrs. Colding's jaw is hanging. I am, unequivocally and gloriously, making a scene.

I don't care. All I care about is the put-upon breath that Adrian draws in, trying to reassert his authority. "*Look—*"

Nope.

"So don't you *dare* rag on her for a few fucking flowers being wilted," I push on. "Are you kidding me?" I'm trembling and giddy with terror, but I won't be stopped now. Something that's been building up inside me my whole life is being purged.

I am a madwoman, eyes blazing, out for retribution.

"I am done with your abuse. I am done with your need to control everything. What happened to your wife was terrible"—Adrian looks away, jaw clenching—"but you need to move on. You want to be human again? *This* is what it means to be human. *Changing.*" And, at last, I soften my voice. "You have to let her go, Adrian. Because there's no room for anyone else in your life until you do."

I stand there panting like a run dog in the following silence. Apparently, my tirade is over. I pick up my peach Bellini and drain it in one go, clop it back on the table. Mrs. Colding shares a look with the other stews, who are watching with mouths ajar. Adrian's throat works, eyes averted. He looks like he's been gutted with a fishing knife.

I suddenly have to get away.

"I think I've lost my appetite," I blurt and turn, but there's a hand on my arm. Mrs. Colding, eyes glistening with something I've never seen before.

Gratitude.

She gives the slightest of nods, and I nod back. *I got you, girl.*

When I leave, hair whipping behind me like some television attorney out for justice, Adrian is staring at the roses on the deck as if he didn't know what they were.

And yet, damn if it isn't hard to not let a smile splash across my face as I march away. The thrill of it, to be alive. To know you've stuck up for yourself, and now that you have, there's no going back.

Welcome to the new me.

Adrian is quiet for the rest of the day. He does not avoid me, though he does not engage much, either. He strolls about the boat with hands in pockets, his handsome face contorted in thought, and it takes all my willpower to not go up to him and try to smooth things over with small talk.

Did I make a mistake, blowing up on him? Did I ruin things?

No. It had to be done.

Mrs. Colding and the other stews, ever attuned to their master's moods, give him a wide berth, nodding to me with solemn, respectful expressions, and even Captain Redfearn makes an appearance to study me.

Something is in the offing.

Dinner is a silent affair, as is the evening basking in the top-deck Jacuzzi, the bubbling water between us feeling like an infinity of distance as he spreads his arms on the edges of the whirlpool and stares out at the panorama of the moonlit Mediterranean, the expression on his pallid face obscured into an enigma by the rising vapors. When he says goodnight, he kisses me lightly on the lips, a strange, wondering look in his eyes.

What is going on in your head, Adrian Voper?

I wake with a start in the early hours. Some instinct tells me I was woken by something, but I don't know what. I look about, half-expecting to see a shadow looming over me, but Adrian Voper is nowhere to be seen.

Adrian.

The feeling hits me: Something is wrong. I need to talk to him.

I'm sweeping the covers back when I see, in the dimness of the master suite, that the curtains hiding the portrait of Adrian's wife are pulled back—but there is no portrait there.

Ah.

I slip out of bed and into a robe.

Somehow, I know where I'll find him. And I do—a lean figure standing on the swim deck, silhouetted against the wake of the *Lair* frothing silver in the moonlight.

He holds the portrait in his hands.

I hang back at the top of one of the staircases sweeping down to the swim deck. Waiting. Heart in throat. Even from here I can sense the coiled sadness, the air of ritual here. I should not disturb this.

Setting the portrait flat on the deck, he touches his wife's face. Then draws out something from the lapel of his suit—a rose. He lays it on the portrait with ceremonial solemnity, and suspending the frame out over the frothing waves—my breath catches—he lets the sea take it.

The portrait rides out behind the yacht on the roiling foam, a square glint of moonlight, and is lost.

Adrian is still staring after it when I creep back to bed, not knowing what to feel.

When I wake the next morning, I immediately sense that something's different. But what?

I prop myself up on my elbows and squint, trying to figure it out. Is it the light? The décor? Warily, I inhale through my nose, testing the air, and my eyes widen.

I turn—and yes, the roses flanking the enormous bed are gone, replaced by vases of gorgeous white lilies.

My jaw drops.

The surprise continues out into the *Lair*. Everywhere, the moody red buds that had ornamented every corner of every deck are gone, swapped with a fantasia of bright white lilies. The difference is staggering. The very yacht is transformed, heady with this new, clean scent. I catch a stewardess passing me with a vase of white blooms. "What . . .?"

She shrugs. "No idea. They were flown in this morning."

And that's when I see a stranger sitting on the shaded bridge deck, reading a newspaper. His crossed feet are bare, his strongly-thewed thighs in shorts, his usual business suit replaced by a billowy white Ralph Lauren shirt.

When Adrian looks up at me, his face breaks into a dazzling smile that robs the breath from my throat. "Good morning, gorgeous."

"Morning," I manage back, feeling my knees go weak, and jump when there's a resounding *crash*—a stewardess has dropped one of the vases.

Heads whirl, bodies tense, waiting for an explosion.

But Adrian, a slow grin hitching up one side of his mouth, sets aside his newspaper and stands. "Nothing to fret over. I think we have plenty to spare, don't you?"

Mouths hang. I turn to see Mrs. Colding, hands clasped before her, standing in the doorway behind me beaming with pride.

A miracle.

Footsteps, and then Adrian is before me, taking my hands in his. "I thought we could have a night out ashore," he says, nodding at the looming magnificence of the Spanish coast. "What do you say?"

What do I say? To the blood singing in me, to the happiness exploding in my veins? To the warmth of Mrs. Colding's glowing approval behind me?

"Yes," I say, the only thing I can say. "Yes. I'd like that."

That. This. *Us.*

All of it, Adrian. I like all of it.

THIRTY

At dusk I consider myself in the mirror, the flirty bodycon dress clinging to my every curve, the earrings shining like stars out of my wavy black hair. I have no idea where we're going or what I'm in for, but I'm all but hovering on my tiptoes with excitement. I'm pursing my lips to apply my signature red lipstick when Mrs. Colding appears like a specter in the mirror behind me.

I jump, but Mrs. Colding merely takes the tube of lipstick from me. I realize she's waiting for me and pucker up.

"Hard to do with shaky hands," she acknowledges.

I laugh. "Yeah." Then, after she traces my upper lip, "Sometimes I still can't believe I'm here. That this is my life now. With Adrian."

The corner of Mrs. Colding's mouth purses in a restrained smile. "I can."

My brow furrows, and she lifts her own in dead-faced seriousness. "Who do you think slipped your résumé to the captain, hmm? Do you think a farm girl like you just happens to get into the running at Lair Yachting, Incorporated?"

I open my mouth, but she tsks. "Lips."

I purse.

"We do a thorough background check on our hires, my dear. And we have our resources. So we wouldn't miss, for instance, any domestic abuse reports you'd filed against an ex." My stomach clenches, but Mrs. Colding looks strangely pleased. "You're a fighter if I've ever seen one. Do you know how long I've waited for someone like you to come along? For someone who had what it took to crack him open?" She studies her work like an art critic, smacks her lips.

I smack.

She nods, satisfied, looks me in the eyes. "You're stronger than you know, Miss Strand. Never forget that."

My throat bobs. "I won't."

After what seems like an eternity she smiles, and my heart leaps. "Have fun, darling."

Mrs. Colding's words are replaying in my head as I emerge barefoot onto the aft main deck, a pair of four-inch heels dangling from one hand. The sun has dropped below the Andalusian Gothic buildings of a Spanish port, and I smell old stone, and palm trees, and hear snatches of Spanish on the cool air. Something whirs, a flash of color gleams in the sky, and I watch with jaw ajar as a crane lowers a flame-orange Lamborghini onto a cobbled street beside a dashing figure in a laid-back blazer. Is that . . . *Adrian?*

His brilliant smile greets me as I descend the passerelle and goggle at the sleek, sexy lines of the sportscar. "What"—I arch a brow—"are you up to?"

But his smile only widens, and he lifts one of the vertical doors open and gestures at the leather-upholstered luxury within. He may as well be ushering me into another world. "Please," he purrs, offering a hand, and I fight back a smile as I lower myself inside and scissor my long bare legs, feeling like a pampered goddess. *Holy shit.*

When he gets in beside me, he levels a look at me. "Ready?"

I nod, heart in throat, and he grins.

When he revs the Lamborghini's V12 engine, the aggressive power of it reverberates down into my bones, taking my breath away. All the needles on the dash leap, and before I know it I'm sucked back into my seat and we've left the *Lair* behind, zooming low along the street cobbles and out into the Andalusian countryside.

Jesus, Arie, try not to get wet already.

We do not speak for a long time. I let his eyes flick over, again and again, to my bare legs, and my chest glows with exultation when I glance over at his lap and see a hard, heavy angle in his pants. He wants me. Now. In this car. His desire for me fills the Lamborghini like a cologne, heavy and possessive. I squirm and squeeze my legs together. I can barely breathe, barely concentrate on the headlights rushing over the strip of blacktop winding through the rolling hills. We must be breaking all kinds of speed limits, for it seems only moments before we're gliding through a high-security gate and a maze of hedge row gardens groomed to perfection. Ahead of us rises a traditional, yellow stucco clifftop villa blasting light and music out over the sea, a fleet of twinkling Ferraris, Porsches and other Lamborghinis nosed into the shade of magnificent cypress trees off the driveway. At our approach, white-gloved valets float out of the shadows as if the night were coming alive.

There's a smile in Adrian's voice when he turns to me. "A friend of mine was throwing a party. I thought you'd enjoy the experience."

I find my voice. "He isn't—"

"No." More serious now. "He's not one of my kind."

I nod and turn to him, trying a smile. "Okay."

He squeezes my hand.

When I'm led inside, my jaw drops for what feels like the thousandth time since I've met Adrian Voper.

So. This is the world of the one percent: a mega-mansion that exudes glamour and soars in every direction, decorated with Italian furniture and antiques and fine art. A DJ presides in a flaring of blinding red strobes at the top of the sweeping staircases dominating the lobby, and techno music throbs in my sternum like the growl of the Lamborghini as the sea of partiers flooding the house surge up and down to the beat. The crowd is eye-popping, filled with the most beautiful people I have ever seen: perfectly groomed men in Italian suits or chic, shimmering Asian jackets, women so stunningly hot they look like creatures from another world as they parade about in bikinis or ruched, glittering mini-dresses, scornfully ignoring the provocateurs dancing in birdcages above them. I suddenly feel like a diminutive impostor on Adrian's arm.

"Why am I here?" I whisper.

"Because you're with me now," he whispers back. "And because you deserve to live like this."

His voice is a rich cognac, filling me with sweet assurance: *I belong here. I deserve this.*

That's right. Screw you, Josh.

"You'll want this," Adrian says, handing me a fluted champagne glass off the tray of a girl dressed like a go-go dancer. Then his head turns. A blonde-haired bombshell with fierce eyes gives him a smoldering look as she passes, and I feel a primal, cavewoman protectiveness flare up inside me.

"*She* has nice hair," I remark acidly.

Adrian makes a face—*Very funny*—and my scowl lapses into a grin as he grabs my hand. "Shall we?"

THIRTY-ONE

We pass through pockets of revelers: elegant European tycoons with girls hanging on their arms and feeding them caviar, Manhattan hedge-fund managers getting lap dances in plush armchairs. I raise an eyebrow, but Adrian tugs me on, leading us through the massive space that opens onto the first floor of the villa. We don't get far. A crowd swarms us, everyone seems to know Adrian and wants his attention. He nods and smiles hellos, charmingly fending off a bright surge of flattery. Instinct overtakes me and I pull back to give him space, but his hand never lets go of mine. "This is Aurora," he keeps saying, and I realize: *He's showing me off.* Unlike Josh, who always hid me from his friends and trained me to grow accustomed to the shadows, Adrian is proud to be with me. *Wants* to be seen with me.

Wants me.

I swallow, flushed and breathless and every nerve ending alight, as Adrian breaks free and leads me on a tour through the house. As far as I can tell, each room is themed to a different form of hedonism. In a gin palace ringed with burlesque girls scissoring their legs in oversized martini glasses, we watch a team of bartenders pour liquid blue fire between tankards and spark cocktails into roaring founts of cinders. In a gastronomy room full of crepe and doughnut stations, we watch a laughing couple cut a cake with a six-foot flaming claymore to the cheers of onlookers. In a dimly lit cigar room full of leather furniture, my eyes bug as men snort lines of coke off the ass of a nude supermodel on all fours on a coffee table. But there's more. A hallway door opens and a horned thing with a billy chin skips out, baaing. A goat. It's a herd of little goats clopping across the carpet, followed by a naked, glitter-dusted woman leading a blindfolded man on all fours by a leash. The man is also naked, his body discolored with bruises and smudges of dirt from the goats butting and bleating about him. My jaw hangs. Then the woman sashays past, slinky and sparkling in the shadowy cigar room, and our eyes meet. A shock. To see a woman here, in power. A woman controlling a man.

That can happen.

Then she's gone, like a dream, goats slipping past like wisps of cloud, and it's just Adrian and I staring at each other, gobsmacked. "Did we just see . . .?" I splutter. And then, "Have you ever . . .?" and Adrian laughs and shakes his head, tugging me on. I stumble after him like a gawking teenager. "This is ri*dic*ulous," I whisper.

"It is," he says, and flashes me a rakish smile. "Isn't it?"

Before long we're threading through the surging bodies in the lobby again. Before long we're dancing, strobes flaring about us. It's a shock to see Adrian dance. I had never before imagined him doing such a thing. But now, nothing could seem more natural. As ever, he is in full command, guiding my body and holding me close with strong, assured hands. Our bodies in rhythm, in perfect sync. Everything in full, delicious contact. We lock eyes, inches apart, feeling the sparks jumping between our lips. *You have nothing to worry about,* his look promises. *You are mine now.*

He bends to say something in my ear. It takes a moment for me to process it over the noise, to understand what he's asking.

Do I want to go upstairs?

I meet his eyes and nod, my mouth dry.

Yes. Yes, please.

He takes my hand and leads me toward one of the sweeping staircases. Heads turn, and both men and women eye me up and down as we pass. "Why do I feel like you're not the only one who wants to eat me?" I comment, in a desperate bid to distract myself from this flood of happiness.

He smiles, and I gulp. *Steady, Aurora.*

At the top of the stairs, Adrian leads me down a hallway and away from the noise. I catch glimpses out of bedroom windows of a pool filled with scantily clad partygoers. In the shadowy bedrooms girls kneel before men, their heads bobbing up and down. A master bedroom is brightly lit and filled with a gymnastic orgy of naked bodies. I'm trembling all over as Adrian tugs me past. "Come on."

I giggle, feeling warm and floaty with tipsiness (God, I'm the cheapest date ever), and he grins as we hurry on down the hall. I should be disgusted at myself, I know. But a small part of me thrills in response to this atmosphere. So many places where we could be alone. And me, with a man wanted by everyone else.

As if to prove this, that blonde bombshell reappears, bumping into Adrian. "Excuse me," she gushes, tucking a sleek curtain of gold hair behind an ear. "I got lost." She lifts her lashes slyly at him and slips by, avoiding my withering gaze. Adrian turns to me, holding a door open to a dark and empty library. "Does this look—"

I stop his words by sucking onto his face and pushing him through the door. He's too shocked to object. We crash against a bookshelf and I tear at his belt buckle, a desperate sound twisting out of me. There is no shyness in me right now, no demureness. I'm all want.

You are *mine*, Adrian Voper—

He pulls back, breathing heavily, and stares into my eyes. Is he—?

"Adrian *Voper?*" a voice calls, and we both turn. Down the hallway beyond the open library door, what must be the host has spread his arms in the gesture of a nightlife impresario. "What on *earth* are you wearing?"

Adrian sighs and turns to me, brushes my bottom lip with his thumb. "Hold that thought?"

I grin. "Okay."

I watch him walk down the hall as I tug my dress back in place. What am I thinking? I must be really falling for him, to so quickly—

"He's a lucky man," says a calm voice behind me, and I jump. A man reposes in a plush armchair in the darkness behind, a vague shape amongst the looming bookshelves. He rises and drifts into a slant of light coming in from a tall window. European, perhaps, or Eastern? Tall, at any rate, with a broody mass of black curls. What was he doing there, sitting in the dark? Was he high on something?

"Is he?" I finally reply, glancing toward the light and safety of the hall.

"He is," the man avers, seeming amused by this. "And so am I . . ." And his lips lift in a smile, giving egress to sharp points. Sharp teeth.

It is in this moment that I notice the form of a woman slumped on the floor by the recently vacated armchair. She is not moving.

The man follows my gaze. "Oh, she just overdid it." He turns back to me, teeth glinting. "Hard not to in a place like this, isn't it?"

And he looks me directly in the eyes.

I take a careful step back. "I—I gotta go," I blurt out.

The man frowns. "So soon?"

"My friend—I should—"

"He wouldn't have left you if he'd wanted you." A pale hand lifts, up and up, toward my face. "Why don't you stay, where you'll be appreciated?"

I jerk back so suddenly I trip and fall on the carpet. The man is frowning down at me as I scramble up, black horror lodged in my throat, and grope away down the hall. Back into light and sound, the blaring music assaulting my senses. I glance behind—just a dark doorway onto the library. No shape following me. No vampire.

Everywhere, though. They could be everywhere—anyone—in this haven of jet-setters.

Why did Adrian lie to me?

A sob catches in my throat. Where? Where is Adrian?

There. The host, in a showy damasked suit. I clutch his arm. "Have you seen Adrian?" I gasp.

The host frowns at me as if I were a crazy woman. "Honey, look around. There are plenty of other sugar daddies here to take care of you."

I stumble back, feeling lightheaded. Of course. Of course he would say something like that.

How else would the super-rich think?

But then Adrian slips out of a door, shutting it behind him. His eyes find me. "There you are," he says, taking my arm. "I got turned around. Are you—what's wrong?"

I'm trembling all over. I grip onto him. "Please get me out of here."

His face falls as he takes me in, and without a word he grabs my hand.

Down the stairs, but there's a firebreather spouting gouts of flame to oohs and aahs in the lobby, so we duck out a side door onto a stone patio overgrown with ivy. The pulsing music cuts off as Adrian shuts the door behind us, and then he's gripping me by the shoulders. "What's wrong? What happened?"

I unleash a wrathful glare on him. "Why did you lie to me?"

His face drops. "What?"

"You said there'd be none of your kind here—"

"There isn't." He turns grim. "Why do you say that?"

"A man—in the library—and there was a woman on the floor—"

"No, no," he soothes, moving to wrap me in his arms. "He couldn't have been one—"

But I hold him back. "How do you know?"

He sighs. "It's hard to explain, but . . . we can sense each other. Almost like a smell." He takes my face in his hands. "I would never leave you alone if one was here. This is a lot to take in, it's understandable that you'd be scared and"—his teeth show in an annoyingly cute grin—"start to see vampires everywhere. You're safe, okay? I promised you: I will always keep you safe."

I want to believe him. I have never wanted to believe anything more in my life. I lift my face, nuzzling at him, and my lips find his. For a moment I breathe him in, as if I could take all his certainty inside me, and then I'm pulling at him with a hunger that terrifies me.

Take me, Adrian.

He does. In one swift movement he drives me back against the ivy cascading down the villa wall, his mouth on mine, so ravenous it draws a helpless whimper out of me. Then his mouth is at my neck, his hands roaming down my sides and up my front, over my breasts. There's nothing polite about it, nothing respectful. It's pure want. The ferociousness of it dumps heat into me. I take the lobe of his ear between my teeth and bite down hard, scrape my nails up his back beneath his shirt, wanting all of him.

Yes, I think. *This again. Please.*

When his hand slides up under my dress and cups my ass, wraps my leg around him, I moan, the roughness of it thrilling, taking my breath away. I've known hands like these. Hands that could bruise and abuse. In fact, they are those hands. The body against mine no longer Adrian's. It's now a body that once reared up above me in the dark as I blinked tears out of my eyes. The face so close to me a blur, focusing into—into—

No.

It can't be, but it is. It's my ex, Josh.

Why? A sob quivers in my throat. *Why am I equating Adrian with—*

A freckling of blood, on the collar of Adrian's white business shirt, gleams in the light from the side door.

The violent explosion of my push staggers Adrian back several steps, his face drawn in confusion. "What—"

"God, I'm so stupid," I hiss. I'm pacing now, jittery and hands in my hair. "And here I was, thinking you were doing this for me—"

"This *has* been for you. What are you talking about?"

I cross my arms and cock one hip, eyebrows raised.

"*What?*"

"The blonde," I finally grit out. "Inside. You found her, didn't you?"

He closes his eyes, shoulders sagging. "Shit."

I shake my head. "How could you? I mean, did you bring me here just so you could *feed*—"

"No!" He slides his hands down his face with a sigh. "Look, I was turned on by you, and—I didn't want to hurt—"

"Shut *up!* Don't you *dare* use that as an excuse—"

"Look, it's not like I slept with her—"

"Oh my *God!*" I scream, holding my hands up like blinkers. "I can't be*lieve* we are having this conversation right now!"

"Aurora, please, I *swear*—"

"I know what it means for you. It's—God, it's like you're cheating, okay? Whether you're fucking her, or"—I throw up a hand—"ripping her fucking throat out. It's cheating."

And we both stand there, feet away from each other, unable to look into each other's eyes.

How? How could I go from every nerve in my body sparking with celebration . . . to this?

I grit my teeth. "I mean, a blonde? A *blonde*?" I half-scream out a groan, fingers clawed and head flung back. "Why? You're with me now. So why the hell are you still going after blondes?"

He opens his mouth—but nothing comes out.

Of course.

I let out an explosive sigh and put my face in one hand. "Look, it's not just that I've already been in an abusive relationship, and I won't ever be able to feel safe with you if you keep doing—*that*. It's bigger than that."

He's the whitest I've ever seen him. He holds up a hand and begins to explain. "I have to do it to someone, in order to be with you—"

"That's not good enough," I snap, and he swallows the rest, looking stunned and tortured.

I suck in a long breath, knowing what I say next will change everything.

"I can't be with a murderer, okay? I just can't. So if we're gonna do this, if you want to be with me—you have to stop." I look him in the eye. "Can you do that? Go on without . . . feeding? Because if you can't—"

"I'll try," he interjects, so sudden it throws me, and I have to wait for him to lift his head and look at me, shining with sincerity. "I've never tried before, but I will. For you."

And we stand there, staring at each other in the private alcove of the patio. In the velvety night above, fireworks begin to pop and explode to the cheers of debauchees, like a sad reminder of our unfulfilled climax.

THIRTY-TWO

I can't sleep. I've twisted my sheets into a straitjacket, tossing and turning in bed, trying to figure out how I feel. We'd sat in silence for the entire drive back to the *Lair*, hands held, suffused with a scared and aching tenderness. And now, alone, the words will not leave me be: *I've never tried before, but I will. For you.*

Screw this, I need air.

I tiptoe abovedeck to witness the sun rise, a wrathful eye cracking the horizon. The air is still shiveringly cool, the *Lair* wet with dew or raindrops in the morning dark. I've climbed to the top deck by the time I notice: overnight, the *Lair* has turned red. My insides constrict, and I peer closer. It's as if some enchantment had been worked upon the yacht while I'd been sleeping. Its gleaming white topsides are mantled in a fine sifting of what looks like—

"'Red dust', they call it," says a familiar voice behind me, and I jolt: Jason has appeared at my elbow. Beyond, in the dawn gloom, figures in white polos and khaki shorts have begun to hose down the yacht. Jason continues as if unaware he'd startled me. "Sand from the Sahara. Wind and rain carry it over the ocean and dump it here in the night." He swipes a finger along a rail and inspects the red grit. "As a yachtie, you never know when you'll wake up and find your world red." He squints at me. "But you know all about that, don't you?"

Anger and surprise blaze up in me. *He knows.* I flip my hair out of my eyes to face him. "You have something you want to say?"

He eyes me askance, gauging my anger, and decides to lead with understanding. "I know you think you know him, but you don't. He won't change—"

"He already has."

His broad shoulders swell in a sigh. "But it'll never be enough, will it? The nature of what he is—that can't change."

"We don't know that."

His lips thin. "Put it this way—you'll never have a moment like this with him." He gestures at the boiling orange face of the sun lifting out of the sea. "You'll never feel safe with him. You'll never stop wondering if, in the heat of the moment, he won't forget that you're not—"

"A meal?"

"Yes." He snorts. "That."

"I know who Adrian is. He promised me he would stop feeding—"

Jason lets out a dry, mirthless laugh.

"—and if he does," I press on, determined, voice rising over him, "I can live with that. I can live with being with a vampire."

He gives me a pained and pitying look. "Then why do you look so guilty right now?" And he strolls away to bark orders at his underlings—leaving me to stare, roiling with confusion, at all that red.

The long, languishing summer days pass as the *Lair* makes its tour around the Mediterranean, dropping anchor in places that belong on vintage postcards: Portofino, Cinque Terre, the Amalfi Coast. Everywhere a blur of ports lined with palm trees and brightly-toned townhouses, sparkling beaches crowded with rows of striped sun umbrellas. I soak up the sun in oiled bliss, and Adrian watches me from behind the safety of shaded windows. At night, we float side by side in the *Lair*'s pool, staring up through the open roof panels at the frothy wash of stars spilling across the sky. We've already found our rhythm.

And always I watch him, like some suspicious wife in a melodrama. But he is unreserved, quick to laugh, his muscular anger and grief wiped away. (Is this who he was before he was cursed?) He stays by my side as often as he can, as if to communicate his loyalty. No surprise disappearances of the stews or himself. No shifty midnight visits ashore. No blonde bombshell snacks.

He is here, with me, and still his new self. Not uptight. Not prone to abruptly firing crew members.

All is well.

Mostly, anyway. The glow of Adrian's fair skin begins to fade, turning chalky and gray, and his grace and power—normally so much a part of him—dims to a strange, halting lethargy. Something in me revolts at what this means and puts it out of mind.

No. It can't be that.

For no matter the stony looks of disapproval from Jason, we glide along as in a dream, Mrs. Colding bustling contentedly about us. An unforeseen blessing, a sweet, steady trickle of underground feeling, making itself known to me: I have never been happier.

Perhaps this is why I choose to tell him about Josh, one night, as we float in the pool.

I tell him everything. The carefree early days that slowly soured into a miserable fog of mood swings and manipulation. The long punishing silences that would make me beg him to tell me what I did wrong. The resentfulness toward my friends that incrementally and methodically cut me off from the world, and which I tried to remedy with a job as a bartender. The ensuing jealousy. The domestic abuse calls. The time I tried to escape, making it onto the bus before the overwhelming reality of life without Josh came crashing down on me and I had to tell the driver to stop, to let me off, let me go back to him.

The time I finally did escape with Cailee, after Josh raped me, and found my way to Adrian.

He squeezes my hand when I'm done. He'd been squeezing it the whole time I'd been talking, turned away from me with his face screwed up. When I lean over and kiss his temple, he shuts his eyes.

"It's okay," I say.

"Why didn't you tell me?" His voice is rough, though not unkind.

"I don't know." I think on it. "I suppose—I suppose I didn't want you to think I was damaged in some way." I look down. "And that I thought of you in the same way as Josh. Given, you know, what you are . . ."

He looks at me then, his eyes strangely bright, and touches my cheek with the backs of his fingers. "I would never treat you like that."

My heart flutters. I cannot breathe. "I know."

He's silent for a moment, staring off at the dark undulations of the sea beyond the pool. "You said Cailee's in France?" he says at last.

The question takes me aback. "Yeah. She finally scored a gig to the Med. Got dropped off in Antibes after a charter." I grin despite myself. "About time. Girl was about to lose it if she had to do another milk run to the Bahamas."

He turns to look at me, a rakish lilt to his lips. "How about we go visit her?"

My jaw drops. "You serious?"

The rakishness reaches his eyes. "We can be there in a few days."

I splash across the distance between us and into his arms, hugging him tight about the neck. "Thank you," I rush into his ear. "Thank you thank you thank you."

He chuckles as I pull back. "Now," he says, and brushes away a wet thread of hair clinging to my cheek. "I'd like to extend an invitation."

I cock my head, squinting. "How mysterious."

His teeth show in a small smile. "Tomorrow night. In the library. I'll see you at eight."

I don't know what to expect. I don't see him all day. Mrs. Colding asks me to keep myself confined to the master suite, and my bewilderment only deepens. *What is going on?*

Sensing the seriousness of the occasion, I choose to wear a modest black dress, do up my hair in a tight, shiny coil that leaves a few wisps to hang down and frame my face. Then I sit on the bed and wait.

When eight finally comes, I'm a jangle of nerves.

The *Lair* is dark when I leave the suite, making me feel like I'm the only one aboard.

But I know that's not true. I know who's waiting for me.

My knock on the door is uncertain, timid.

"Come in," Adrian calls.

I have to blink for a moment, taking it in. The library is ringed in candles, pockets of glowy light amongst the book spines. Adrian stands by the baby grand piano in a dressy shirt, an unsure smile on his lips. Seeing Adrian unsure is almost as scary as seeing his fangs in a woman's neck.

"Thank you for coming tonight," he says. I don't know what the look is on my face, but it makes him glance at the piano and hurriedly add, "This isn't about Evangeline." He locks eyes and gestures to a chair. "Please."

I throw him a skeptical look and sit, hands in lap, doing my best imitation of Mrs. Colding. His right cheek dimples in a smirk and he seats himself before the piano, lifts his hands. I suddenly realize I've never actually seen him play.

His fingers descend into a gentle opening chord, and I hold my breath at the beauty of it. It's a declaration. No anguishing minor key here, no melancholy. This will be different.

And it is. It begins slowly, with a rolling bass hand and a tentative, probing melody, like a soul searching for light. He has not played this before; this song has never haunted the *Lair*'s passages and hallways. The music swells, and Adrian bows over the keys, lost in the emotion of it, his fingers pounding the ivories with godlike ravishment. He is like a romantic figure in a storm.

I am happy, the music says. *I am tortured with happiness, now that I've found you.*

I have composed this for you.

Heat gathers behind my eyes, my throat constricts. It is almost too much to bear. The music soars, up and up, into a thunderous climax of stirring tenderness, and my heart swells. I undergo a wave of pins and needles.

For something is happening. The revelation is splitting me like lightning, tipping me into a state of disarray, harrowing and blinding and transcendent.

I. Am. In. Love. With. Adrian. Voper.

The tears are spilling out of the corners of my eyes and down my cheeks when his fingers falter in a dissonant jumble of notes.

Adrian stares at his hands, scowling, and tries again, tapping out the melody. But his hands betray him. He lifts them up to find they're trembling.

His face slackens. He touches his brow.

I stand, a sputtering of words on my lips:

That was beautiful.

Is that how you see me? Is that how you see us?

I need to tell you something—

But before I can get closer he jolts upright, knocking the piano stool over, and I flinch. He touches two fingers to the piano to steady himself, his face raw, and frightened, and frighteningly pale.

"I—I'm sorry. I have to go."

I lift a hand. "Adrian—"

"I'm sorry," he says again and fumbles at the hidden staircase door, disappears.

Leaving me to stare after him, wondering what in the hell just happened.

I do not see him all the next day. He is conspicuously absent from mealtimes, and no shadow ever darkens the windows when I sunbathe at the bow. An expedition to the underwater observation lounge reveals a cold, empty space full of wavering light reflections, and no Adrian Voper anywhere.

On the second day I find Mrs. Colding on the sun deck. She lies on a lounge chair, hands crossed on her stomach, staring out to sea. The sight of Mrs. Colding lying down—of not *doing anything*—is utterly unnerving.

But I step forward. "Where is he?"

She spares me a sidelong look, returns to contemplating the Mediterranean sparkling like ground glass. "You don't know?"

The defeat in her voice constricts my throat.

"Where . . . where is he?" I say again, trying to keep the tremble out of the words.

Mrs. Colding turns now to give me her full attention, her pinched and immaculate face radiating scorn. "He's not taking visitors right now, dear."

My arms break out in gooseflesh, but I lift my chin. "Where. Is. He?"

Mrs. Colding opens the door to the VIP stateroom and steps aside in chilly invitation.

It's pitch dark within, giving shape to nothing but a stiflingly hot void, as if it were den to some beast raging with fever. Perhaps it is. "Be careful," Mrs. Colding intones, and waits until I look at her. "He's hungry."

Something cold flows through me, and I waver in place.

No, I think to myself. I love him. I trust him. That would never happen. He would never allow that. Think of him tending to me, in this very room, during my bout of food poisoning. That's all this is. Me returning the favor.

Everything all right, babe?

I slowly advance into the dark room.

It takes a moment for my eyes to adjust. The light from the open door slashes toward the bed, giving just enough light for me to make out its vague immensity in the dimness. And the form atop it.

It shifts.

"Adrian," I whisper, feeling the hairs on the back of my neck rise.

More rustling. The form turns away from me. "Go away." His voice is a croak. "Please go away." I realize, belatedly, that he's shivering.

"You have nothing to be embarrassed about," I say, edging closer. "I just want to look at you . . ."

His next sentence stops me cold. "I can smell your blood."

I clench and unclench my fists, willing my breathing steady. Then reach out one hand to his shoulder, the other to a bedside lamp. "I know you won't hurt me . . ."

It happens in the same instant: the light switching on, and him whirling to me, pale and sunken and mouth crowded with fangs, his gorgeous eyes bloodshot, and I think of a rabid animal gone mad with bloodlust.

I'm sobbing and tripping and bounding to the door and it's slammed shut behind me, Mrs. Colding locking it with a sad, knowing expression as I break down crying and I hear Adrian's voice on the other side, pleading with me, *Shh, it's all right. Just give me time. This phase will pass. We'll get through this.*

We'll get through this.

THIRTY-THREE

This is what I hold to. He's not dying. He's already dead, right? It's just withdrawal; he's going mad from lack of blood.

We'll get through this.

"Has any of his kind ever tried this before?" I ask Mrs. Colding. "Is it even possible for them to not have blood?"

Mrs. Colding's hands are clasped, her face composed in an imperious mask of disapproval. "Not that I know. It's unheard of."

"So, we don't know what will happen?"

A pointed shrug.

Later she approaches the door, raps softly on it. "Adrian?" A sigh, like a disappointed schoolteacher. "Adrian, you don't have to do this. Maybe we should—"

"*NO.*" The roar from the other side of the door is like a furnace blast, and Mrs. Colding jerks away, lips pressed together. I cannot stay there. I back down the hall, hands clenched, repeating it to myself: *We'll get through this.*

But Mrs. Colding snorts at this. Her scorn is limitless.

"You could talk him out of it, and instead this is what you cling to?" She shakes her head. "I thought you would be good for him. Now look at you. Killing him."

His rages come next. Smashing the furniture, cursing, howling. The crew begins to talk, congregating in the passageways or hurrying by the VIP suite with worried looks. What is on this boat with them?

Mrs. Colding, recognizing the danger, declares the aft section of the main deck off-limits. Mr. Voper is sick and has quarantined himself. Nothing to be frightened of.

All is normal.

I keep to myself, sitting numb and alone in the pool or at the long dining room table. I cannot eat, cannot sleep, hunched over with sharp pains that are like a hammer hitting me in the belly. All the while, Mrs. Colding and Captain Redfearn consult amongst themselves in whispers. Jason gives me odd looks.

I do not care; I do not speak to anyone. I wrap myself in my seclusion, like a grieving widow gone mad with desolation. I shut my eyes and pray for the first time in my life. I pace endlessly in the master suite, hands balled and trembling with little whimpers of anger and complaint, wracked with crying spells and indecision: *I am killing him. I am saving him. I am killing him.*

After two weeks, I have to—I go to the door. "Adrian?" I call.

The smashing halts.

"Adrian, maybe Mrs. Colding is right." I lay a hand on the door, as if taming a wild thing. "I'm sorry I asked this of you. Maybe—"

"Just a little longer," comes his rough reply. "I think . . . it's almost done."

"Okay," I say, nodding and blinking away tears. "Okay."

The next day, the rages stop. The stateroom is silent as a tomb.

"It's time," says Mrs. Colding, and gives me a look. "I know you'll do the right thing."

This time, I crack the door slowly. Waiting. Listening. My whole body braced and ready.

No response from the darkness.

"Adrian?" Nothing. My heart is lodged up under my breastbone, against my ribs, pounding away. I edge the door wide enough for me to slip through, and leave Mrs. Colding waiting in the hallway.

There's almost a mustiness in the room now, a faint sense of sickness and decay amongst the ruins of smashed furniture. The air is stale and close, making my brow perspire. I swallow. "Adrian?" I chance again. "Babe?" I can just make out his form on the bed, the faint gleam of sallow skin. The sheets are pulled down to his waist. "I'm going to turn the light on, okay?"

Still nothing.

I reach out a trembling hand, fingers skittering against the lampshade, and switch on the light.

I cannot bear to look at first. I keep my eyes shut and my body rigid, waiting for the spring of fangs, for the snarl of an Adrian I do not recognize—but nothing happens. And so I peek my eyes halfway open.

What I see makes me clap a hand to my mouth.

The transformation is shocking. His smooth ageless face has sucked against the skull, eyes squinted pinpricks in the glare of the light. His beautiful body—once so splendidly formed—has wasted away to a bundle of spindled limbs, parchment skin cloven to the laddered palings of his ribs and his hands hooked to display blackened talon-like nails imprinted into grayish flesh. If set on a scale, he wouldn't weigh more than eighty pounds.

"Hi, baby," he whispers, chapped lips splitting as he smiles weakly up at me.

There's a sharp indrawn breath; Mrs. Colding has drifted up to my shoulder. She lifts her chin in a brittle gesture of renunciation. "I am done," she declares in a hoarse voice. "Whatever this is, I will not support it any longer. You're on your own."

Footsteps, and the door slams, snapping my eyes shut and starting a tear streaking down my cheek.

So. This is real. This is happening.

"It's okay," Adrian husks with a faint smile, one of his withered hands reaching feebly for mine. "She's never gone . . . for long."

But it's not okay, Adrian. Nothing about this is okay.

"You're . . . you're *dying*," I manage, my lip beginning to tremble. "And I *let* you. I *asked* you . . ."

This is what it has come to. My entitlement, my need to be loved. This is what this new me can demand if I am not careful.

Or perhaps all along, all along, I have been this way.

"Hey." Adrian's voice, penetrating this suffocating vacuum. "Hey. Listen."

How can I? How has the world not cracked wide at this moment?

Yet, somehow, I am sitting on the edge of the bed. Somehow, I am holding his hand as he speaks. "You've always pushed me . . . to change. To make me . . . better."

I swallow down my rising gorge, to seal in that howling pain.

"This is merely . . . the last step. Freeing me . . . of this." His lips quiver back in a papery smile, that smile that can ransack me top to bottom with happiness. And he says it, the words I never expected to hear: "I love you, Aurora."

My eyes instantly fill, the words echoing in my head: *I love you.*

No. Don't say that now. Don't make this real.

You. Being taken from me. Forever.

But his eyes close, that smile still on his face. Is he . . . gone?

My heart turns over.

"Adrian?" I shriek. "*Adrian!*" And the noise comes out of me—*No-no-no-no-nooooo*—as I press my brow to his, rocking back and forth as I let out great wracking sobs of despair, as if purging something from my body. But I can't stay there. A harsh pragmatism forces me away, I have to stand and think, hands to my head. I have to make this right. How can any of this be made right?

It can't. I have tried to make him into what he isn't, and have killed him for it. He has killed himself for me.

I am pacing and sobbing and clutching myself, calling his name.

Adrian. Adrian.

I'm sorry, Adrian.

Forgive me.

Restore me to a previous time. Before I asked this of you. Before everything.

And then arms are around me—warm, living arms—and I start. It's Jason. He must have heard, must have known. The door to the suite stands open behind him, no sign of Mrs. Colding, but his face—tanned and freckled by the sun of the outer world—is drawn in concern. "Hey," he says. "Hey, what's wrong?"

"Adrian," I sob, and point. "You have to help me . . ."

But when he stands over the bed and studies a seemingly sleeping Adrian (how do you know when the undead have died?), he shakes his head. "It's what he wanted, isn't it?"

"Yes, but—" I sketch at the air. How does he not understand? "It's my fault—"

His face falls. He places his hands on me again. "It's not your fault. Never think that."

That does it. I break down again, and he shushes me, rubbing my arms. "It's okay. It'll all be okay." He is close, and warm. He lifts my chin—it seems so natural—and his lips are on mine.

The room quivers. "What—"

"Shh." He is calm, frightfully calm, as if explaining the best method for buffing out a stain on a boat hull. "It's for the best. He's a monster, Arie. Let him go."

His lips again.

I push at him. A fearful dryness has attacked my mouth and throat. "This is wrong." But his hands won't let go of me. He pulls me against him. "You know what he is. What he was. The world is better off without him."

My blood chills. My tongue moves like a wad of wool. "Jason, what are you—"

His hand trailing up my leg, under my dress. "I'm here. I was always here . . ."

"Get off!" I push at him—hard—and his face darkens. It's a silly-looking face, really, I don't know why I've never noticed that before. That dorky, appealing handsomeness full of vital effort, a strained sunniness forever verging on a sulk.

But it's gone beyond sulking now.

The blow is astonishingly painful. A stinging numbness follows, spreading across my cheek, and I'm still stumbling back when he mutters it. "Fucking bitch. I'm the good guy here, Arie. I was always the good guy, and you chose *him*."

So. This is where the danger was, all along. No bloodsucker, no creature of the night.

Just a man pretending to be a good guy.

He grabs at me again, and the familiar terror sets in like a paralyzing poison, shutting down my brain functions. I know what comes next. The self-preserving submissiveness, the floating disassociation. My consciousness leaping into a nearby object—a bedpost, a door handle, the weave of a rug—so I can watch what is happening to me from a detached distance, as if it were a scene from someone else's life.

You taught me well, Josh.

But I don't feel that this time. This time I feel a great upwelling of unfairness, of disgust at my helplessness, obliterating all thought.

This time I feel rage.

I claw out, a sudden raking of my nails that draws blood, and Jason snarls and his next smack sends me crashing into the wall. I try to knee him in the groin, but he pins me brutally against the nightstand and yanks my legs apart, bumping the lamp and sending shadows leaping as he gropes at his belt buckle, his breathing harsh now, mechanical and full of hate.

Nothing, then—nothing at all—has changed.

The old animal terror is screaming through my veins and out of my skin when I'm abruptly released.

I drop to all floors, dazed, and look up to a sight that refuses to conform to logic: Jason's feet. Jason's feet, suspended in the air.

The pale, withered shape of Adrian is standing above me, lips snarled back and eyes hazed a ferocious black, his clawed white hand somehow holding a flailing Jason in the air by the neck.

Awe sweeps through me.

Jason's head suddenly snaps to the side—*crack*—and his body goes limp. A thud of dead weight and Jason is staring at me, one cheek to the carpet and one arm folded under him at an unnatural angle, his eyes wide, glazed, and full of horror.

Adrian sways, and when our eyes meet for the briefest of moments his face gentles—and he drops to the floor, the light leaving his eyes from that final expenditure of energy. My whole body stiffens.

"No—no!" I scramble over, and Adrian's eyes droop as I cradle him. "Don't you leave me, Adrian Voper. Don't you *fucking dare!*"

His eyes laze open—and droop again. My stomach freefalls. Panic descends on me like a shroud. What will keep him here, in this moment? What can I say?

What I've been longing to, for so long. What I've been holding myself back from saying.

"I love you, Adrian."

It comes out as a low, throaty sob, and so I say it again, louder. "Do you hear me? *I love you, goddamn it!*"

That does it. His eyes fight open; I see bright sclera and the gorgeous blue that thrilled me the first moment they lit on me. I laugh brokenly and smooth the limp hair back from his face. "That's right. You come back to me now. Come back to me."

A faint smile spreads across his features—and his eyes shut again. Not enough. Too far gone. There's only one thing that can bring him back now.

Jason is still on the floor, feet away, his eyes craned at me in his paraplegic state.

A numbness expands in me. The words echo in my head: *I cannot change what he is.*

When I press Jason's wrist to Adrian's mouth, his nose takes the scent of skin and blood immediately—but he restrains himself.

"It's all right," I whisper, the words ragged. "Please. Do it. For me."

A long, long pause. And then Adrian clutches the wrist to him as his mouth opens to do its work.

I sit there, lip trembling, and stroke my lover's hair as he nuzzles into flesh, a warm wetness soaking into my dress.

I cannot change what he is.

It takes him half an hour—an hour, an eternity—to slake his thirst. By the end Jason is as drained and pale as a cavefish, and multiple times Adrian vomits blood onto the carpet, so frenzied is his feeding. By the time he lets Jason's wrist flop from his smeared mouth, he is bloated and near insensate with satiation, hooded eyes fluttering.

I wrestle him into bed and lie back beside him, my hands at my heart, and try to reconcile how I've gotten here.

Back where I started: lying in terror beside a man I cannot change.

My fear is so intense that a great calm descends upon me, a cleansing mercy that leaves me clear-eyed and resolute. Next steps simplify in my mind, arrange themselves into manageable impossibilities.

Think now: He is what he is, that cannot be resolved. And you would never forgive either of you if you stayed with him.

You have saved him, though. There is that, at least. You can go on, content in knowing that he is out there, somewhere, even if it means you are apart.

Even if it means you cannot be with him.

I shut my eyes, my bottom lip trembling. Do not let the howling grief come. Wait just a little longer, until he is asleep, for your escape.

You've done it before, after all.

Hello, sun.

Slipping out of bed and to the door, thinking, *Do not look at him. If you do, that will be the end of you.*

Returning to the master suite and changing into a clean set of clothes, grabbing my purse. Enduring the moment of racketing terror when I steal out onto the main deck, not knowing if there'll be a deckie out on watch. The air is crisp and cool, Antibes' Port Vauban with its high medieval walls still a vague shape in the dawn gloom. I cast one last look about for any crew members astir and dart to the passerelle, onto the dock, away.

It's happening. This, here, is happening.

I'm leaving him. Like a thief in the night, I am leaving him.

And I feel it, the thought nosing to the surface like the maw of a shark, bright with disaster: How will my life ever progress from this moment? Why would I want it to? Everything has split open, and there is nothing to be figured out anymore.

I'm sobbing when I call Cailee, she can barely hear me through my grief.

Come. Please. Please come.

Stumbling about through the stone arch of the harbor and clutching my stomach as if it had been sliced open. *Adrian, my Adrian,* I croon to myself, over and over, the words a cherished wound.

THIRTY-FOUR

Cailee is staying in a sort of crew house in the chic resort town of Juan-les-Pins, a twenty-five-minute walk from Antibes. Which means I have twenty-five minutes to do what I have to do.

It all seems so simple and straightforward: I must forget Adrian Voper. Store away our time together, packed up like so much treasure, so that I will never again bump into it and be waylaid.

This, surely, should be easy. I've done it before, after all.

But it isn't. It's impossible. Because this is a different thing, isn't it? An altogether different thing. He is not like Josh, to be easily banished and turned, in my mind, into a stranger that I'll be able to look back on years later with a puzzling fondness or detachment, wondering what role he ever played in my life.

No. Adrian is not like that. He comes back to me in wave after wave of overwhelming recollection—his voice in the submersible, the first time he laughed, lifting away the blindfold to show me the Northern Lights—and I know he will never stay in his proper place, set aside and done with. I will suffer through these memories, jolting me unexpectedly and with varying degrees of intensity, for the rest of my life.

I am crying again when Cailee finds me sitting on the stone bench by the harbor, and I'm smelling her rich cinnamon hair and she's stroking my head as she rocks me, wrapping me up in sisterly assurances: *He was a jerk. This'll pass. They're all monsters in the end.*

I am on Cailee's recovery regimen now: shrug it all off, keep everything at bay with a steady dose of bright busyness.

First on her list: emotional eating. She leads me away from the waterfront haunts of the local yachties—"*Ooooover iiiiiit*"—and through the narrow, cobbled streets of Antibes as if she's lived here all her life. She's a full-blown tour guide. Her wrist flicks as she points out tourist traps, underground absinthe bars, men to avoid. Everything a blur of painted shopfronts and lamp posts hung with explosions of flowers (were those roses?). I'm about to pass out from dizziness when we end up in a square full of warbling pigeons and an ornate merry-go-round of dubious functionality. In short order we're sitting outside a café, legs crossed and watching vacationing celebrities and trophy wives with glossy shopping bags pass by (was that a Hermès logo?) as we devour crepes smothered in whipped cream, Nutella and almond flakes. Cailee keeps flicking glances at me, and I know. She's waiting for me to tell her what happened.

I want to. I want nothing more than to pour my heart out, unload everything so that she can do her calm, analytical post-mortem on the relationship, as she always does, so I can make peace with it.

But I can't. I can never tell Cailee why I left Adrian. I can never tell her, my best friend, what he is.

What, then? I sit on this secret forever, in crushing isolation. Even if it hurts her. Even if it hurts our relationship. And then what? How can I go on living my life when I know what I know now? A demon world behind this one, grinning through the cracks, turning such everyday things as shopping bags and fucking flowers into objects of dread.

A couple catches my eye. A slender woman flushed with youth, an enormous diamond on her finger, and a slightly older man in shorts and Ray-Bans peering at jewelry in a shop window. I watch the man place a hand on the small of her back and wonder how long it'll be before their marriage opens up, like a trapdoor, and she sees the grinning fiend in him, the many leering violences of masculinity. At least with Adrian, I had known what I had. What pitfalls to navigate. His appetites purified into comprehensible, externalized horrors. With men—with normal men—that was not the case. That was not the case at all.

There I go again. Still holding on to the positives in a relationship. Still unable to let go.

Attagirl, Arie.

It's mid-afternoon when we check in to the Royal Antibes Hotel. Cailee, bless her, made reservations for us before meeting me so I don't have to stay in her party animal crew house. She has to lead me about by the elbow, as if I'm lost in a black hole—time is blurring and curving like light, moving on without me. Life is moving on without me. The flamboyantly uniformed baggage boy keeps glancing at me in the elevator, and my stomach turns—the mere thought of attention from any man besides Adrian makes me sick. Then our room door is shut and locked, the "Do Not Disturb" sign swinging from the doorknob, and our girls-only breakup recovery getaway officially begins.

I don't remember much of that weekend. Days spent lolling in bed in fluffy white bathrobes, painting each other's nails and laughing like maniacs, ordering room service while we watched TV. Then the hours of Cailee holding me as the sobs welled up, the waves of obliterating grief washed over me.

On Monday she wakes me. She has daywork and needs another hand. I should come along.

"G'way," I moan into my pillow.

"Arie. Honey. It'd be good for you."

"Ugh, *fine*," I huff, rolling over and blowing out air at the ceiling.

Anxiety prickles through me as we approach the harbor. Is the *Lair* still there? A small, childish part of me sulks at the fact that Adrian didn't hunt me down, that I never heard a knock on the hotel room door and found Mrs. Colding waiting chilly and impeccable in the hallway, ready to escort me back.

But Adrian wouldn't do that. He would respect my wishes.

What would I do, though, if I bumped into Mrs. Colding out here on the dock? Would I give in?

I'm spared this conflict. The yacht Cailee and I are washing down is moored inside the harbor, away from the *Lair* at the outer quay for the bigger boats. This results in a whole afternoon spent doing a washdown while forcing myself not to look over at the *Lair*.

Cailee, mercifully, switches to full gossip mode to distract me.

"You were right, these rich yacht owners?" she says as we squeegee bridge deck windows. "All the same. Sucking bottles and fucking models."

Or sucking models, in my case.

"I mean, the yachts are just extensions of their dicks. Why do you think they're always comparing the lengths of their boats? '*Mine* is a hundred and fifty-*five* meters,'" she mimics in a dry British accent, and snorts. "But Corsica, right? I mean, Bonifacio? All those cliffs and cobbled streets? A-*maz*-ing. And you wouldn't be*lieve* how hot the guys were on my charter. Like, *mega hot.*

There was this engineer from Jamaica, and this one time I bumped into him in the engine room . . ."

But I can't tune into it. Adrian tumbles through my brain, smiling at me and then turning into a desiccated corpse with blood bearding his chin—

"Babe!"

"Huh?"

Cailee looks at me with patient understanding, squeezes my arm. "We're all set. I'm gonna talk to the captain, okay? Get our pay. Maybe see if I can get us hired for a charter trip."

"Yeah, sure. Of course."

I nod, trying my best smile, and she pads down the teak gangway still damp from our wash, dips into the wheelhouse with an uncertain look back at me.

Get it together, Aurora.

I coil up the hose, set about drying up the last of the puddles on the deck. I'm wringing my mop out into a bucket when I see it: a smudge of blood, tiny and inconspicuous, on the hatch of the anchor-chain locker.

Oh. Oh crap.

Panic buzzes up in me like wasps, and I think, *It's nothing. You're just being paranoid. After Adrian, you think all blood has something to do with that. All yacht owners can't be them, right?*

It's just . . . sportfish, perhaps, a marlin or tuna stowed away after a catch.

But in an anchor-chain locker?

I look about to make sure the decks are clear before lifting my mop out of the bucket. One step at a time, Arie. Hold the mop at your side. Creep forward. You'll be laughing about this in a minute.

My heart is clamoring up into my throat when I shriek up the hatch and peer down.

It's a small space, the anchor-chain locker, but big enough for someone to fit inside. New deckhands—or "greenhorns," in yachtie speak—usually get the unenviable job of climbing down into that stifling dark and "flaking the chain." That is, spreading it out in great loops as the anchor is lifted so it doesn't get tangled up. But the body I see splayed out on the small mountain of rusting metal doesn't look like a greenhorn who got trapped and forgotten down there.

I know because it's the body of a young woman, and her head is flopped back to reveal a pair of fang marks crafted into her throat, her pale face frozen in an expression of utter horror.

Aurora, meet yesterday's dayworker.

I take three small, staggering steps backward, overturning the plastic water bucket in a spray of soapy water. Suds foam about my bare feet. My eardrums boom. The breath whistles in my lungs. At the bow jackstaff, a flag—faintly familiar—ripples in the wind: two inverted white triangles on a black field.

A chill of vague recognition seeps through me. And then I remember: *Cailee.*

THIRTY-FIVE

My heart lurches. Adrenaline shoots through me in a chemical cascade, bathing my brain in a fizz of dread. I brandish the mop like a baseball bat and hesitate before the door of the wheelhouse, thinking of bodies writhing in bedsheets, of a corpse dropping to a bone white deck. I open and close my hand to get the jitters out of it, and yank the sliding door wide.

No one there in the wheelhouse. Maybe I was only—

Thump. The sound is distinct and irrefutable, coming up a short set of stairs.

The hairs on the back of my neck rise. An urgency takes hold of me, a sudden certainty: Something is happening down there.

I have to move. *Now*.

I fast-pedal down the stairs.

A crew galley waits at the bottom, cramped and gleaming with stainless-steel surfaces. It's also dim—the lights flicked off, the window curtains drawn to block out the glare of day, a golden haze along their edges.

It's like stumbling upon a pit of vipers.

There's a man down here. He's not close. He presses himself against a far wall in the gloom, his eyes rounded in his stolid, double-chinned face, his gut hanging out of his captain's shirt sucking in and out in a series of short, labored hitches. He's staring at the thing crouching in the floor, its pale skin contrasting against the gleam of its sharp executive's suit: the yacht owner. Cailee lies unconscious at its feet, a patch of blood glistening at her scalp; it must've just knocked her out. At my last, stuttering step, the thing lifts its head. Its eyes are deep and black and without pupils. When it hisses, a pair of fangs drip saliva like some venom-beaded serpent.

The moisture dries in my throat.

I lock eyes with the captain flattened against the wall, trying to engage him in a pleading look: *What are you doing?* But he only twitches his head in the negative and half falls, half slides away along the wall and is gone.

A sickening astonishment takes hold of me, an appalling urge to laugh.

By myself it is, then.

I look down to see the owner-thing's long spindly fingers tilting back Cailee's neck, baring the beating thread of an artery, and my blood cools.

I'm not sure how it happens—I cock back the mop and let fly with all I've got, whipping its head to the side. When it slowly turns back to me, an ugly gash in one brow, its opaque eyes are slits and its lips wrinkled back like an animal's.

Shit.

Its backhanded swipe lifts me off the ground. There's a pop in my ear, a wrenching pain in my neck, and the world blurs. Then I'm crashing over the crew table into the far banquette in a heap, as easily dismissed as a fly flicked off an arm. I hear a crunch in my spine, and there's a dull, warning throb in my shoulder I don't like at all. When I get my breath back, I can taste hot vomit in my mouth.

In the next room, a swaggering man's voice is suddenly advising to not stop him from having a good time. The captain's turned the radio on.

Cailee, I keep thinking to myself. *Cailee.*

I open my eyes, and this viper's nest suddenly seems to vibrate, distorted and endlessly replicating. As I watch, the owner-thing splits in two, then comes back together. It hisses—a ferocious, territorial sibilance—and turns back to Cailee.

My blood sizzles.

I try to get up, and the room slews violently to the right and I fall back down. It's much easier to let a dark wave of familiar thought sweep over me, lulling me into doubt. I have, as always, been cast aside. This is where I belong. I don't deserve any better. My whole existence, after all, has been contaminated with worthlessness. Why would that change now?

The voice in the other room croons he's gonna keep on going, there's no stopping him, and I think, *No.*

I get a flash of Josh above me, pinning me down with one hand as a clenched fist connects, over and over, with my cheek.

Not again.

Jason pinning me against the nightstand, groping at his belt buckle.

No more. This will be the end of that chapter.

FUCK THAT.

I wince up, looking about, and an endless sequence of sticks collapses into a single mop. *My* mop. Still miraculously within arm's reach.

I do it without thinking—I stomp down on the wooden handle, snapping it in two so that I'm now holding a jagged javelin, and plunge it with all my strength into the owner-thing from behind.

Full impalement.

It arches back and shrieks, and time seems to slow, the air filling with a red mist that sprays all over the gleaming silver surfaces of the galley in an exultant and obscenely beautiful ballet of gore. All I can do is blink and wonder, stupidly, *How long will it take the stewardess to clean all that up?* And then the thing has thrown itself to the floor and is crabbing about on its back, bucking and flailing as it ululates like some unholy abomination. A calmness settles over me, a kind of blinding, cleansing fury, thrilling in its liberation. It does not occur to me that I may have arrived at some unbearable and ecstatic truth about myself, a willingness to deal in solutions where others might balk. *It was simply what had to be done*, I may think later.

Now, all I think is, *Why won't it die?*

The solution presents itself: a row of hefty knives stuck to a magnetic strip above the stovetops.

At the end of the row, black-handled and all business, gleams a cleaver.

THIRTY-SIX

After I manage to haul Cailee up the stairs into the wheelhouse and out of sight of that place, I shake her awake. "Cailee. Cailee."

She blinks and jerks, eyes wide. "What—"

"I can't carry you down the passerelle. Let's go."

She glances down the stairs, to where she mustn't look, and touches her scalp. "Fucking *asshole*," she breathes. "Did he—?"

"*Now*, Cailee."

She follows along in a black temper, finally tries to jerk away. I only allow her once we've made it onto the safety of the sun-drenched dock.

"What the *hell*, Arie?" she shouts, red-faced. "What happened? The owner—what did he—"

"Cailee."

She stills at the flatness of my tone, her face paling a little. "What?"

I sigh and grip her shoulders. "Do you trust me?"

Her eyes move between mine, back and forth. Her reply, when it comes, is soft and unsure. "Of course."

"Then fly back home. Walk away from this industry, and never look back."

Her jaw hangs. "*What—*"

"Just—trust me, okay?"

"But—*why?* Our *dream!* This was our big escape together!"

I nod, solemn. "I know. This is me looking out for you—"

Cailee snorts at this. "I don't—Jesus, so what if one creep—"

"*Cailee.*" The word lashes like a whip. "I won't be able to sleep unless you do this, okay?"

She swallows and backs away now, shakes her head. "What's going on?" She takes in the splash of blood on my white polo, my stony composure, and narrows her eyes. "What happened to you?"

I draw in a long breath, thread a hand through my hair. "I don't know."

Cailee's eyes sheen with tears. "Arie, you're freaking me out here . . ."

"Oh, babe." I take her into my arms, and she holds on to me, trembling. "It's gonna be okay," I soothe. "I just—I love you, and I want to know you'll be safe."

"I love you, too." She pulls away, rubbing at one eye, and sniffs. "Will *you* be safe?"

She doesn't need me to answer; the look on my face is all she needs. A small, wondering smile hitches up her mouth as she takes me in. "What am I gonna do if I never have to worry about you anymore?"

I crack a bittersweet grin. "Live for yourself, babe."

It's only when I say it that we both know it's true. This has been our dynamic for as long as we've known each other, ever since that first day we met at summer camp and instantly began comparing the moles on our backs, our dramas at home, and set about—in the unfussy, unspoken way of young girls—figuring out who would take care of whom for the rest of our lives.

Tears of pride are glistening in Cailee's eyes as she looks at me. "So what are you gonna do?"

When I look out of walled Port Vauban to the millionaires' quay beyond, the *Lair* is blazing like a deadly mirage in the sun.

Mrs. Colding is waiting for me on the aft main deck when I get there, hands clasped, hair gleaming in the sunlight, like a replay of our first meeting. As if she somehow knew I would return.

By the time I'm at the foot of the passerelle she's met me there, and we face each other on the baking dockside for a long moment.

"He'll be happy to see you," she states at last. There is no emotion to the words. This exchange has been drained of all drama like some ritual or ceremony.

I nod. I know.

She steps aside, gesturing, and slipping off my shoes I walk bare-footed and straight-backed up the familiar telescopic gangplank with its hooped handrails—passing, once more, into that other world.

I'm almost there when she calls back to me. "Thank you." I turn, and she settles her face into a new expression, overcoming some internal reluctance. "For what you did." She lifts her eyes, and there's that conspiratorial look again, that respect given to a peer. Or even a friend.

I nod again, mouth quirking.

Inside the *Lair* all is silent, seemingly vacant of crew members. When I come to the door of the VIP stateroom, Jason's body is gone. A refurbishing crew in white coveralls is laying down a new carpet, overseen by a brooding Captain Redfearn. He catches sight of me and stills, his broad forehead creasing as if weighing something—what my role here means, perhaps, and how it will affect his boat—and juts his chin aft.

The master suite, then.

One of the huge red doors is ajar, as if beckoning. I take a deep, measured breath, and crack it all the way open.

He sits scrawny and alone at the end of the massive bed in a business suit, like a boy in his father's clothes, his hands slow and clumsy with the buttons. Girding himself in his armor once more. Bespoke protection for his broken heart.

I broke his heart.

"You know, I preferred you without the suit," I say in a soft undertone.

He jolts to his feet, as if caught in the act of something private and shameful. With him upright, I can see his body has begun to reverse its queer wasting process, and though still thin and gray-faced he no longer looks like a skeletal starveling.

Such swift, such astonishing enchantment.

Only took a gallon of Jason's blood.

At last, he gets it out. "You came back," he says, sweeping unthinkingly at his brambly hair.

"Yes." The word hangs in the silence like a stone.

He tries to pull himself together. "Aurora, I—"

"I saved my best friend's life today," I calmly cut him off. He blinks. "One of your kind was gonna have her for an afternoon snack."

He swallows and slowly sits down again—out of shock or weakness, I can't tell which. "I'm sorry." Then he notices the blood on my shirt, and his eyes go round. "How exactly did you—"

"I'm sorry, too," I say, stepping into the room, and study the bare spot on the wall where his wife's portrait once hung. "I realized she'd never be safe in this industry. In this world. And that I would never forgive myself if anything happened to her."

He watches me, uncertain. "Aurora—" he tries again.

"You protected me, Adrian, when I needed it most." I whirl on him, stopping him cold. "Just as you promised. But I know now. I don't need you—or anyone—to protect me anymore."

And I reach behind me, lifting up my shirt, and untuck the bloody cleaver that's jammed into the band of my shorts.

Adrian's jaw hangs. The effort to understand on his face is so cute it's unbearable. "Aurora, what—"

"I could never fix the abusive men in my life, because you can't fix that kind of wrong. But I can fix your kind, Adrian."

He waits, very still now, alabaster brow furrowed. "What are you saying?"

I stand over him, chin lifted and cleaver flashing, and he stiffens. "You said you can't change back to a man unless the vampire who turned you is killed?"

He nods, slowly, eyeing his nervous reflection in the mirror-bright cleaver blade.

"Well." I brush his hair back with a mother's care, letting a devious smirk curl my lips. "Then we're gonna find that bloodsucking bastard"—I lightly menace the air with the cleaver—"and chop his fucking head off."

He stares at me, taking it in. The audacity of it. "But that head is the head of our coven. No one even knows where he is—"

I grip the scruff of his neck and pull his head back, stop his words with a kiss I've never given any man. A kiss that screams possession. A kiss that burns.

When I pull back, his eyes are wide, amused, and marveling.

"We'll find him," I promise. "If we have to pick off every last vampire, one by one, to draw him out, we'll find him. And we'll make damn sure they never harm anyone again." I let the cleaver fall—*thunk*—point-down and quivering into the floor so I can hold his face with both hands, my forehead to his. "Because you're *mine*, Adrian. And I'm not going to lose you. You gonna help me?"

The import of it hits him now. The plan. What I'm saying. *Us*. It's as if centuries-old shackles fall away. His face changes, and that light comes out of him again, those dazzling smile lines spreading wide, filling the whole world to express one huge, emphatic word:

Okay.

ACKNOWLEDGMENTS

When I hopped a bus to Florida to become a yachtie all those years ago, little did I know I was to write this book. Only later would I think to put Dracula on a yacht, and populate this world with all the yachties I met along the way. So thanks must first go to everyone at the Crew Castle, and to all the other crews in Florida and the Med. Thank you to my early readers, Rebecca Mlinek and the Writing Gang, who saw this book come together chapter by chapter. Thank you to Pily Gonzalez-Diaz for encouraging me to fully embrace what this story is and put more "meat" on it. Thank you to Trif Book Design for the amazing cover, and to my editors, Mary Yakovets and Beth Hale, who made the story inside shine. But thanks most of all must go to Dava, my most trusted reader, whose contributions cannot be overstated. I couldn't have written this book without you.

ABOUT THE AUTHOR

D.V. Sullivan has been a deckhand in the Mediterranean, a bartender in New York and an English teacher in China. Now that he's no longer hosing salt off yachts during high-wind gales, he writes from his lair in the Pacific Northwest.

DVSullivan.com
Facebook.com/AuthorDVSullivan
TikTok @dvsullivanauthor
Instagram @dvsullivanauthor
X/Twitter @bydvsullivan